CREVASSE

Clay Vermulm

ISBN 13: 978-1-915399-03-8 (paperback)
ISBN 13: 978-1-915399-04-5 (e-book)

Clay Vermulm | www.clayvermulmfiction.com
City Stone Publishing | www.citystonepublishing.com

Printed: April 2022

DEDICATION

To my parents, Roger and Kendra, who always encouraged me to pursue my dreams, even as they were wishing I'd get a normal job.

and

To my wonderful wife Deanna, who supports me in every conceivable facet of this writing journey.
I could not do this without you.

THE MAN IN THE RED COAT

Aside from the swirling wind revealing itself in sheets of powdery snow, the only sounds on the towering mountain peak were the clicking and scraping of steel on rock, the punching of an axe into ice, and the deep, steady breathing of Travis Jayden. Alone amongst the stark greys and whites of the upper Picket Range, his bright red jacket stood out like a fluorescent spot in the near-arctic terrain. Slowly and methodically, he ascended the treacherous Inspiration Peak.

As a solo alpinist, Travis's pack wasn't full of bulky cams to secure himself to the wall; where a standard mountaineer pack contained over a dozen ice-screws for protection on the ascent, Travis brought only three for his single rappel. A static seven-millimeter rope was coiled in his pack, along with a harness, a foot of two-millimeter utility cord and figure-eight belay device for emergencies only. For instance, if this thin veil of powder, riding a moderate alpine wind, evolved into a howling blizzard, as it often did in this rugged terrain.

Aside from his emergency 'bail' gear, all he brought to the mountains were his essential climbing tools and provisions. On his feet were stiff-soled mountaineering boots, to which he'd tied his steel spiked crampons for purchase in steep snow and vertical ice. He wielded a small, technical ice axe in each hand, sharply curved and pointed at the bottom of the handle to stab into deep snow.

Travis took a few testing swings into an overhanging shelf of ice above him. It was no thicker than his torso, but it hung in a long sheet, a cascade of fallen water frozen until the sun would undo the work of the frigid altitude in the coming months. After the third swing of his axe, the sharp serrated steel stuck solid. He inched his spiked boot onto a thin ledge of rime-coated granite and kicked it into the ice. Setting his right-hand axe over his shoulder, he leaned back, gaining a better view of the route above. Ahead, the frozen cascade continued to a large, exposed patch of black granite. Its white speckles sparkled in the greyish light of the overcast sky.

Switching his grip on the axe, he shook his left hand, giving it a rest as he gazed over the glacial valley below. A broad smile creased his cheeks as he inhaled the beauty of the Northern Cascades unfolding for him and him alone. In all his years climbing the Pickets, he'd scarcely seen another soul, and when he had, they'd been fellow mountaineers. Few others would suffer the arduous trek to this forgotten range for climbs that were not only difficult but largely uncharted and dangerous. Looking down, Travis had no fear of falling, no apprehension at his remote and virtually un-rescuable location; all he felt was the all-encompassing freedom of being the only human within twenty miles.

The alpinist shook each arm once more, wiggled his fingers and toes to promote blood circulation through his rapidly cooling extremities, then took his second axe back up to continue his ascent. Click, click, click, tapped his axes, testing the ice before he committed the tools to the heavy swings which thunked in for purchase. A swing of the axe, two steps of the crampons. A swing of the axe, up two steps, and on he went toward the top of Inspiration Peak.

Travis was climbing the first ascent on the south face of the coveted peak, following the line of a sheer face towering over an obvious snow gully. The path of frozen ice sheets and snow cornices would guide him up a more gradual snowy field to the top, after he cleared a section of exposed rock. Now, having reached the granite section, he sat on a ledge about as wide as a pickup tailgate and prepared for the most gut-wrenching section of the route.

Though often used on ice features that could crumble off to plummet into the valley below, axes and crampons did afford excellent holds when one knew where to stick them. He'd always been most nervous soloing on rock, with nothing but his shoes and hands to keep him on the face. Miranda, Travis's girlfriend of the past six years, constantly gave him flak for this, as it was "contrary to any sane climber's logic to trust frozen water more than solid rock." He smiled. *Good thing Miranda can't see me now.*

He thought of the hundreds of climbs they'd done together. Miranda had met him at the crag for their first date. Since, they'd climbed all across Washington, in Yosemite Valley, and even in the crumbly sandstone canyons of Zion. She was a bold and competent climber, but he'd never managed to convince her to solo climb with him. She deemed anything without protection "suicidal and asinine." So, for the sake of preserving their relationship, he'd stopped asking her to come on trips like this. He loved her, and he loved solo climbing. Without one or the other, he wouldn't have felt whole, and though he felt the occasional pang of guilt at her worrying over his safety afterwards, during the climb, there was no room in his mind, body, or soul for anything but focus.

As Travis looked up at the rock face, he applied climbing chalk to his hands and inhaled deeply, all errant thoughts of home, his partner, his obligations, fading. He began to climb, and the world outside his route evaporated like water on a hot sidewalk.

* * *

He was the rock beneath his fingers. He was the alpine air. As if floating on the wind, his movements were graceful in their entirely calculated intention. The void of jagged scree and crevasse-fractured ice yawned below him with its majestic yet menacing presence. Many climbers speak of the call or pull of the void, of being reminded of fear and consequence, should they make a fatal error.

Travis felt none of that. If his foot slipped, he reacted quickly, securing handholds, locking his other foot, and making sure to get the unsecured appendage on the best feature available. If he grew fatigued, he found a crack or jug in which he could lock a knee or leg to take the pressure off his feet and hands. When he felt gravity tugging, or the wind buffeting him, all he did was smile wider. He'd always remind himself, or anyone who questioned his sanity on the subject of soloing, going up is the easy part.

* * *

Travis reached the top just as the sun reached its zenith. The route took him about seven hours, excluding the five-hour approach. The cloud cover, which had overcast the majority of the morning, was burning off, revealing the mist-veiled valley and sweeping ranges around him.

He removed his cell phone from his pack and pushed the power button, hoping the cold hadn't frozen the components. It wouldn't be the first time he'd pissed off his sponsors by failing to document a notable ascent. At the back of his mind, he heard his publicist chiding him. "VID-EOS, Jayden. People want VID… E… OS. You've heard of a little thing called TikTok, right? Or do you not get cell service amongst your rocks?" *For a first ascent on the south face of Inspiration, I guess I better take a damn picture.*

The phone finally powered up, and he turned the video on. "Hey Jan," Travis said into his iPhone 5 camera. Keeping that shitty phone for nearly a decade was another thing both Miranda and Jan hounded him endlessly about. "No service up here, but it seems like I can still take one of those videos you're always going on about." He flashed his most winning grin.

"I'm here on top of Mount Inspiration. Yee-haw!" he shouted in exultation as he panned the camera around to show the Picket Massif to the east and west and the Cascades stretching toward the northern and southern horizons.

"And I got here by climbing *that*." He angled the camera over the edge, leaning out over the dizzying heights, seemingly without a care in the world, to show the sheer ice, rock, and snow face he'd just ascended. He returned the camera's focus to his face, so the pinnacle of Mt. Inspiration was visible over his left shoulder. "I'm naming this route Miranda's Nightmare. Love you, baby."

Again, he flashed a winning grin, panned around one more time, this time keeping his bearded face in the frame as he let out an echoing, lupine howl up to the midday sun. "Now, I just gotta get down." He arched his eyebrows at the lens and then angled his camera to the relatively low-angle ridge line of his descent path. "Wish me luck," he said and stopped recording.

That'd have to do for Jan. TikTok videos were capped at ten seconds, so the way he saw it, he'd just created two weeks of content. Enough to collect a paycheck, right? Besides, accomplishing the climbs was his real goal. The interviews with *Rock and Ice* and *Outside* were what would put his name into the hat for a *Reel Rock* documentary, not his fucking TikTok.

With a sigh of relief, Travis turned his phone off and stored it back in the depths of his pack, where it would be happily forgotten. He drew out the rope, harness, and figure-eight belay device. He sat down, geared up, then stood to sling the rope over his shoulder and begin the slow plod down the snowfield. The rocky ridge line arched like the spines of some colossal slumbering dinosaur, weaving downward toward the valley floor.

Hiking down the increasingly steep slope, Travis sunk to his knees in the deep snow with every step, forcing him to pull his feet nearly to his chest for the next stride. By the time he reached the granite spires of the ridge line, where he could use the sparse gear he'd packed for a rappel, his core and thighs were aching as if he'd run a marathon. He took a few moments to breathe the spring air; CO_2 puffed out in wispy clouds. He let the thin, biting-cold oxygen fill his lungs before continuing his journey.

He twisted a large ice screw into a thick plate of ice, secured his 120-meter static line to it, and ran each side of the rope through his figure-eight. Using a small line of cordelette, he created a backup Prusik knot in case something should cause him to lose hold with his brake hand.

After testing the security of his system, he stepped over the edge and dropped toward the waiting glacier. Travis hit snow at the bottom of the wall, about a quarter-mile to the east of where he'd begun his climb. As he pulled and coiled his rope, he surveyed the glacial traverse that awaited him. Glaciers were the parts of the mountains nobody ever talked about. Even mountaineers didn't usually bother warning others about the dangers of glaciers because, until you've been on one, it doesn't compute.

When inexperienced eyes look out over a glacier, they see a relatively flat plain with some icy ridges and rises that protrude from the snow. Compared to a sheer mountain face, two thousand feet above the safety of solid ground, a glacier doesn't look particularly impressive or intimidating. What inexperienced eyes don't see is that glaciers are peaks between the mountains under the snow, often descending thousands of feet. Tucked beneath the more prominent features of the surrounding mountains, the glaciers hide, silently waiting to swallow the unwary.

When Travis looked out over a glacial field, he felt a bit nervous. A small part of him worried about the high probability of happenstance. He knew many a skilled mountaineer had fallen into a crevasse or been in a glacial valley due to a crushing avalanche. No matter how good an alpinist, there was little to nothing they could do in those situations.

He packed everything into his bag, strapped on his mountaineering boots and crampons once more, and pulled out his trekking poles.

With another deep breath, he headed out. Just as he reached the ice's edge, he stopped.

A large, lumbering black shape on all fours, with a noticeable limp, was standing in the middle of the glacier. As Travis stared, it seemed to notice him. It turned toward him, standing up on its two hind legs as if to gain a better view.

A bear? This time of year, bears could be seriously bad news, as they would be ravenous from hibernation. Travis didn't know a hell of a lot about bears. He'd seen a few in his years among the mountains, but he'd never had any close or frightening encounters. Too small for a grizzly, it looked like a black bear, but it was still larger than he was comfortable with. He looked down the valley, trying to focus on his destination. *Just get moving, it'll take off,* he assured himself as he crunched out onto the hard ice of the glacier. Trying not to think about the bear, he prodded the ground before him with his trekking poles, taking each step deliberately where he found solid ice.

The Terror had always been a relatively crevasse-heavy glacier, but with rising temperatures over recent years, the ice had begun to melt at faster rates. Like a still patch of river has fast-moving currents and undertows hiding beneath, a snowy glacier often belies treacherous six-hundred-foot canyons that terminate in caverns of broken ice and sub-arctic pools. Travis knew that what felt like a solid patch of ground could sometimes be a cornice no thicker than an inch, only still in place because no idiot had come along to walk across it for centuries. *If you happen to be said idiot, well, you might be going for the last big ride.*

Prod, step, prod, prod, step, and so it went as he made his sluggish way across the glacier, all the while keeping his eye on the hulking black bear that still hadn't moved. The very fact unsettled Travis. He started to wonder if it was one of those life-size decoy animals people put in their fields.

It'd be a hell of a job to hike that out here just for a prank that no one's likely to see. I guess people do weirder things. But he had seen it moving before, hadn't he?

Thoughts of crazy people and hungry black bears fresh from hibernation continued to loop through his head as he drew nearer to Washington's largest land-based predator. He'd had enough wilderness training to know the general rule of thumb for a brown bear or grizzly was to play dead and hope it loses interest; for a black bear, get big and scare it off. This was a principal he'd heard from experts but had never needed to put into practice, thank God. Any other time he'd seen a black bear in the wild, it had been from a way off, and as soon as it saw him, the animal would move. Of course, most of those other times, the bear had been in a more populated area. *So, why is this damn thing still here? Maybe this guy isn't as used to seeing people. Maybe he doesn't know how dangerous we can be.*

To punctuate that thought, Travis stowed a trekking pole, reached over his shoulder, and snagged one of his ice axes. Holding the wickedly curved, razor-sharp instrument gave him a sense of security. Though he had no idea how effective his axe would be against his ursine opponent, he would make it pay if it wanted him for dinner. As a lover of fantasy fiction, he had always harbored a secret desire to go down fighting with axes high against some seemingly unbeatable foe. Upon nearing the bear, the world melted away.

All he heard was his heavy breathing, the clicking of his crampons, and the crunching of his trekking pole as it plunged through the snow to hit solid ice. On his last prod, the most crucial connecting-with-solid-ice sound was chillingly absent. He stopped and took a deep breath.
He poked to the right, the left, searching for solid ice on which he could move forward.

The bear was still there, frozen as a statue, now only two hundred yards to his right. He prodded farther left. Finding a bit of ice, he took a cautious step in that direction before being forced to stop again. As he searched a path before him, he realized he was all but surrounded by a hidden gap beneath the snow. *Shit.* Had he stepped onto one of the thin cornices he'd just been thinking about? His gut clenched as the reality of having no control over what was beneath sunk in. The difference between him making it out of these mountains and plummeting into an icy chasm to his death sat upon the balance of this ice shelf of indeterminable stability.

Travis took a few deep breaths, focusing on what he *could* control. He had footing beneath him, solid ice behind. One step after another and he'd be back on track. He took a few steps backward, scouting the left edge of the cornice, though continued to find nothing but loose snow which crumbled into the open air below it. The mountaineer glanced again at the bear, at the direction he'd be forced to walk in. *Well, I hope Yogi isn't feeling feisty over there.*

Yogi certainly didn't look feisty. He looked dead. *I'm convinced I saw that damn thing moving before.* Travis wasn't sure which was more intimidating. Reluctantly, he started walking toward the creature, maintaining his attention to footing. The path to his right began to solidify. *Why did you have to stop right there, you creepy bastard?*

Two hundred yards became one hundred. As he neared the beast, he was startled to realize that its muzzle and underbelly were splotched and stained with a reddish brown. The bear also had a large portion of his face missing on the left side. A gleaming white section of jaw and broken teeth was visible through tears in its greenish, rotting flesh.

One hundred yards became fifty. The creature seemed to stare at him with unblinking black eyes. Or were they staring through him? Maybe this thing really was dead, implausible as that seemed with it sitting tall on its haunches. Maybe it had passed from the realm of the living before his eyes.

Just as he was finishing that thought, it cocked its head.

"Please, don't…" a woman's voice begged. The timbre was weak, exhausted, desperate, as it trailed off like a fading echo. The voice paralyzed him. Bile rose in his throat. He would have dropped his axe, were it not tethered to his wrist. He was only reminded of its existence when it swung down and poked into his leg with its sharp point, causing him to flinch back to reality.

"Please don't…" the creature repeated as it dropped to all fours and faced him. No exhalations puffed forth from the partially decayed jaws of the monster, yet it made deep huffing noises as it stalked toward him.

Its heavy paws sank deep into the powder, generating alarming creaks in the ice below.

"HEY," Travis shouted, holding his axe and pole above his head. He waved them and extended his arms to make himself look larger. The neon red of his jacket flashed brightly in the sun. "GET BACK! STAY BACK!"

"Please, don't..." The bear continued forward with that slight tilt of its head, dead eyes surrounded by mangy, flaking skin, and fur coated in what Travis was now sure was dry blood. *Oh fuck*, he thought as the bear turned its slow stalk into an increasingly quick lumber, closing the distance between them faster than he thought was possible.

Frantic, Travis didn't think. He just reacted. Axe held high, he waited until the bear was a foot away and swung where he estimated the creature's head would end. It still plowed into him, hurling him back onto the snow and ice with a sickening crunch. Vision swimming, Travis tried to gasp, but could get no air into his empty lungs with the terrible weight of the creature atop him. The beast, luckily, was not gnashing him with tooth and claw. It was not rending his flesh from his bones or smashing his rib cage into splinters with its two tons of muscle. It wasn't moving at all.

Travis heaved and shoved and squirmed his way free from the bear's girth after an arduous struggle. By the time he emerged from beneath the reeking creature, he was forced to lie in the snow, panting before he could gather the energy to stand and consider whatever the hell was going on. *Did that just happen?* He realized it had indeed. Somehow, he didn't even seem to have broken anything. *Holy shit. I actually did that.*

His one strike had connected absolutely perfectly with the center of the bear's skull. The axe had sunk so deep; even after several straining, wrenching attempts to remove his trusty tool, he was forced to leave it embedded between the beast's eyes. As his adrenaline ebbed, he began to grasp the disturbing reality. *None of this makes any sense.* In all his years up here, he'd never seen a bear, not once.

Even stranger was the fact that no heat steamed off the newly made corpse. It lay there, stiff and still. Already, it seemed as if it had been dead for days, especially with its appearance of decay.

Despairing at the loss of an axe that had carried him up countless summits, Travis was, nonetheless, itching to get as far from this strange creature as he could. He turned and started following the bear's tracks across the snow toward the far edge of the glacier at a fast clip. Still cautious, Travis prodded for crevasses and took mindful steps, but the assurance that his forward path had already been tested by a fully grown bear allowed him to move with more speed and confidence.

As he blinked tears from his eyes and his breathing stabilized, the red haze of adrenaline faded. *Five hundred feet, and I'll be off this damn glacier. Free and clear.* He set the goal firmly in his mind and focused his vision forward. Until…

"Please don't…"

Travis froze. Cold sweat burst from every one of his pores as he slowly turned around. The bear was standing on two legs. This time, it approached in an impossibly fast, bipedal sprint, with the axe jutting from its head.

As it picked up greater speed, it dropped to all fours and loped. Travis screamed, turned, and took off in a desperate dash, still following the tracks. Without realizing, he'd dropped his trekking pole into the snow.

Unfortunately for the seasoned mountaineer, there was no preparing for a circumstance like this, no matter how experienced he was. The tracks didn't lead to the edge of the glacier. Instead, they led to a yawning crevasse. He didn't see the gaping, icy blue canyon stretching down into the depths of the glacier and spanning at least twenty feet across until it was too late. Suddenly, he was leaping for all he was worth, but such maneuvers only work in movies. His hands weren't remotely strong enough to arrest the velocity of a fully committed plummet toward the earth.

Travis barely had a chance to scream as he vanished into the blue void below.

* * *

In the mountains, miraculous things happen. Sometimes, seasoned veterans are killed by random rockfalls. Others fall into ice caves with floors covered in jagged, broken spears of rock and ice and survive. Somehow, Travis had landed in the one section of the crevasse that was full of soft, fluffy powder.

As improbably good as his landing had been, it had not saved him from grievous wounds. When he tried to stand, a jolt of agony lanced up his leg and spinal column, and he dropped back down. He lay on his back, gritting his teeth almost hard enough to splinter them, and sucked in a violent breath before screaming. The cry echoed off the icy walls, resounding as if in an empty theater.

It was dim and silent in the crevasse. A deep oceanic blue seemed to glow from the walls. Travis could scarcely make out a thin slit of light streaming into the corridors of the glacial cavern, but even that seemed to be fading. He studied the waning light, wondering how long he'd been down there.

Concerned he'd passed out at some point and knowing he might need to be rescued, he reached into his pack and searched for his cell phone. Ironically, the thing he hated bringing to the mountains above all might be what could save him. When he found it, however, he could tell it was pulverized. It fell into three pieces as he extracted it. Travis let out a manic laugh which transformed into the desperate sobbing of a doomed man as he lay there, alone, hoping to freeze to death before that bear, or whatever the hell it was, found a way to get to him.

* * *

The bear never showed up. Neither had the freezing to death. Travis had no idea how long he'd been at the bottom of that ice cave. Somehow, he was still alive. He remembered reading Joe Simpson's story, a man who'd fallen in a crevasse in the Andes and managed to climb out and descend the mountain on his own, without the use of one of his legs.

If he could do it, maybe I can, too. That'd be a story to secure his place in the local climbing lore. He wouldn't have any trouble pleasing his sponsors if he could pull off a miraculous survival like that.

Axes high, he thought as he willed himself to his feet. Well, he tried. He was able to get weight onto his left foot but putting any amount of pressure on his shattered right one sent a crippling pain throughout his body like a blast from a taser.

He could tell by the sickening angle of his leg that it was broken in at least one place but right now, all he had time to focus on was trying to get out of there. Determined, he pulled his remaining trekking pole from his pack and used it to lever himself onto his good foot. He shivered uncontrollably as his blood started to flow once more. Inching his way slowly, using one wall of the icy canyon for support, he squeezed through a narrow gap in the ice and rounded a small bend. He searched for any feature or slope he might be able to ascend with his limited gear in his weakened condition.

It was then Travis realized the light he was seeing had not come from above. It was coming from the narrow corridor in front of him. A pale bluish-white glow seemed to emanate from around the next bend. He supposed it was possible for a crevasse to lead to the bottom of a glacier somewhere near the ground. Though he'd never heard of such a thing. *A way out?* He knew a huge glacier like the Terror had networks of tunnels beneath its icy surface; he hoped, against all odds, that maybe he'd fallen into the exact right crevasse for survival.

Rounding the corner slowly, he saw a flash of movement from inside the large chamber before him. Travis stopped in his tracks. Leaning against the wall, he stilled his breath to listen. He heard faint voices. It sounded like several people, speaking in frantic, confused, or desperate tones. He identified at least seven distinctly different voices. As he took another step, his head swam with a concoction of pain and delirium. He could hardly see for the dots and flashes of white and black that flooded his vision. Each step felt like breaking his leg all over again. He wished he could just hack the damn thing off and be done with it.

Shuffling further into the opening, Travis scanned the chamber. It was tall and semi-circular, almost too perfectly shaped to be carved by nature. The faint light he'd seen was glowing from within this room, it seemed, from within the very walls. As his vision cleared and his eyes slowly adjusted to the mysterious light, he saw the vague silhouettes of several figures standing around the edges of the chamber. The conversation increased the longer he peered into the room. No, not a conversation, seven or eight voices, repeating phrases.

"Please, help me!" a man's voice shouted.

"Why are you doing this?" asked an older-sounding woman.

"You…" a man said with dreaded recognition.

"Hello?" Travis asked, hesitantly stepping around the corner. Part of him wanted to hide, but a larger part, the part that ached to see Miranda again, to hug Jan and laugh about his stupid video with her, that part wanted desperately to survive. These were people. They could help him.

All the voices stopped when he entered. Travis's stomach dropped in terror. He wanted to scream, wanted to run, wanted to do anything, but he was frozen, transfixed. From behind, he heard heavy footsteps.

"Please don't…"

TWO MONTHS LATER

QUINN

Quinn's legs quivered with fatigue after finally getting the tent back in place. She checked to see if they'd lost anything. They hadn't, so far as she could tell. Once again, she began hammering in the stakes.

Yeah, yeah, smirk at me over there, she thought, turning her gaze to Greg. She knew he was watching her in his peripheral vision. Her bare, lithe shoulders flexed as she knelt in the snow, tending to the task. The high-altitude sun beat down on her exposed skin, beginning to turn it a little pink. When they'd arrived at camp, she and Greg had been so sweaty and exhausted that they'd immediately stripped to cool down. Better to dry off while it was still sunny than have it turn into a cold damp when the sun went down. She'd learned that lesson the hard way on her first climbing trip with Greg.

Right now, Quinn was at the tail end of another such lesson. She'd set the tent up and arranged everything the way Greg liked it. Things had to be just so, or the first thing he'd do was to take everything out and rearrange it himself. The only thing she hadn't done was stake the tent.

"The weight of the gear should hold it down," she'd insisted.

He had smiled and shrugged. "I'd stake it down, but that's just me."

Not ten minutes later, Greg had been gathering wood for the fire and Quinn had been squatting in the snow with her clothes pooled at her ankles, when a huge gust of wind ripped off the mountains and blew their tent fifty yards down the slope. Greg had doubled over laughing as she scrambled to get her pants back on and rushed to the tent's rescue.

"Ah, yes, a truly wise decision," Greg said now, flashing a teasing grin. It was one of her favorites, and the bastard knew it. It was also the perfect complement to his newly affected, sublimely subpar British accent.

"Yeah, yeah," she muttered.

"Staking down the tent in these harsh mountain conditions," he continued, smoking an imaginary pipe now, "Most earnestly advised."

Quinn rolled up a snowball and pelted him right in his cocky, sarcastic face.

He came right after her, lifting his knees high in a clumsy pursuit through the snow. She screamed in fake terror and attempted to scramble up the hillside, but he was faster. Catching her, he pinned her down, but before he could secure her arms, she grabbed a firm hold of his nipples and raised a threatening eyebrow. Greg slowly let go and raised his hands over his head as if she were pointing a revolver at him. "Now, let's not do anything drastic here... nobody needs to get hurt." To his credit, he was still trying the accent.

"I agree," she said, giving his nipples a gentle twist. "Beg for mercy, and I might let you live."

"Mercy, Lady Quinn, oh please! They've scarcely tasted life!"

She pushed him aside and stood. "See that you remember this. Next time, they shan't be so lucky." Her accent was significantly better than his.

Quinn walked away with a smile and ducked her head into the newly staked tent. The thin nylon flapped about in the wind, but inside it remained surprisingly insulated from the frigid mountain air. It always amazed her that this magical fabric could mean the difference between life and death in an alpine environment. Quinn quickly reorganized the various items that had spilled from her pack and unrolled her inflatable sleeping pad. She opened the valve on the side of the pad and began inflation, and then she did the same for Greg's. The pads sucked in the crisp winter air and dutifully held it. Quinn dipped back out of the tent and zipped shut the flap to keep in the warmth. Greg sidled up next to her.

"All you had to do was admit I was right," Greg said, chuckling. "Is that so hard?"

She rolled her eyes and shook her head. That was all he deserved. Greg smiled and turned toward the mountains, pulling on his lightweight jacket.

Quinn surveyed the campsite they had chosen. Just below, dominated by tall, swaying pines, was the tree line. Above loomed the Southern Picket mountains. It had taken them over six hours to get to the wide, shallow bowl but the pure isolation and beauty had been well worth it.

While she'd been rescuing and reorienting the tent, Greg had gotten a nice fire going in a pit of stacked shale. He ducked into the tent and emerged with their small propane stove.

Setting it safely away from their fire pit, he filled it with snow and ignited the gas canister to make fresh water.

"I can't believe all that gear didn't hold the tent down," Quinn said.

"That would usually work, but we're at six thousand feet, and the wind really rips off that glacial valley up there," he explained. "The tent is basically a parasail here." He showed his painfully genuine smile. She loved that smile. No matter what he said, the smile always said *I love you.* "Don't feel bad. I never staked down my tent until I had one blow off a cliff on me."

She laughed. "You never told me that."

"I wanted you to think I was cool." He stood back up and said over his shoulder, "I'm gonna saunter over to the glacier and see how it's lookin'. I'll be back in a bit."

"I'll have dinner on by the time you get back. Holler if you need me," she replied, digging into her food supplies as the snow in the pot melted into the cleanest water on earth. She untied her hair, letting the long, tangled knot of brunette curls tumble free. She put her fleece-lined beanie back on and grabbed her jacket, shrugging it over her goose-pimpled skin. *Climbing is an amazingly enlightening sport, but why does it always have to be so cold?*

Perhaps it was the earlier mention of the glacier, or the isolation and encroaching darkness, that made Quinn nervous. Sometimes when she was feeling anxious before a trip, or when she was waking up in the subzero darkness of an alpine 3 a.m., she would ask herself, "Why do I do this on purpose?" Other girls her age were playing university-funded sports like volleyball. Those girls relished the social prestige, the adoration of a crowd, and the roar of applause. Quinn savored the sheer and epic glory created by the natural world. Every time she camped in the woods or made it to the top of a mountain, she knew the answers to her doubting questions. *I do this because there is no feeling like this in the world. The mountains are another world, here only for those who put in the effort.*

Never mind that when people reached the top, all that awaited them was cold wind, exhaustion, and a looming descent. The joy and satisfaction of accomplishing a hard climb could never be imitated by the fleeting adoration of college sports fans. Adoring crowds would fade into distant memories, like those her dad and his drunken navy buddies would recall when reminiscing the 'good old football days.' The mountains and the rush after a climb would always be here for her.

Quinn heard the water begin to boil and pulled out baggies of dehydrated beans and packs of ramen. She dumped the beans into their bowls and added the water, covering them with a couple of flat rocks to let the beans steam to life. Then she rolled over a large rock and sat in front of the fire.

Around fifteen minutes later, Greg tromped back into camp. By then, the sun was dipping below the tops of the craggy peaks, casting them in a pinkish-yellow glow. His large climbing pack with its protruding ice axes made him look like a windswept mountaineer who had trudged into these savage wilds long before paved trails and catwalks and volunteer-chiseled stairs adorned the paths to the peaks.

But one look at a real grizzled mountaineer would make it clear that Greg was from an age of cell phones and apps that guided him to even the most secluded places in the world.

Quinn had no room to talk, of course. She'd spent most of her life avoiding dangerous activities, and thus was decidedly un-windswept. It was only in recent years that she had gotten the 'outdoors itch.' Despite Quinn's preppy looks, she was stronger and tougher than most gave her credit for. She'd spent every day at the climbing gym and every weekend out in the mountains for the past two years. Now she could outclimb many of the men at the gym. Climbing had turned out to be the perfect sport for her logistic-focused, research-driven mind. It required technique, finesse, and homework, and she could do the hell out of some homework. Strength and tenacity were key for prolonged enjoyment, but research was necessary to succeed and stay safe.

Greg, on the other hand, was all grit and toughness, the exact other side of the climbing spectrum. He'd been raised on the values of Mark Twight and Fred Becky: dirtbag camping, free and clean traditional climbing, and, of course, 'don't be a pussy.' Not much of a planner, Greg never thought into the future further than a week unless he was organizing a climbing trip.

At school he'd been gregarious and a bit of a class clown. He'd been captain of the college climbing team, handsome and reasonably clever. He was also well aware of these traits. People usually didn't say no to him, and he was accustomed to achieving his goals, as he'd been doing in the mountains since he was a little boy. Before Quinn had gotten to know him, she'd figured he was a complete douchebag. He was always striding around campus with that self-assured gait and cocky smile she now loved, doing the bare minimum at everything, but somehow still succeeding.

Until Greg had seen her at the climbing gym, he had never said a word to her, even though they had a class together. But they'd hit it off, climbed a few routes together, and now they'd been dating for nearly a year. In that time, she'd learned that Greg could definitely be a bit of a douchebag, but he was also kind, funny, quick to laugh, and most importantly, he was genuine. Quinn had realized that Greg's academic laziness stemmed not from a lack of motivation but from a lack of interest. His goals had little to do with academia, and college was simply an obligation to him. She now saw his cocky smile as merely a personification of the child-like enthusiasm with which he lived his life.

When Quinn noticed Greg approaching, she added the ramen noodles to their bowls, then replaced the rock lids and promptly strapped on her headlamp to help him navigate. Anxiety loomed over her like a storm cloud over the sea. Tomorrow would be her first multi-pitch alpine climb and, hopefully, a first ascent of the unclimbed north face route. First ascents were coveted goals for any young climber, but this one had become an obsession for Greg. Tomorrow would also mark Quinn's second glacier traverse; the first had been a disaster.

She looked down at the ice axe jutting from her travel-worn pack. The pack was like a faithful companion: it had carried her burdens through hikes, crag climbs, bouldering, and even a kayaking trip. The ice axe was foreboding, formidable, and proud, like a holy weapon she did not deserve to wield.

She hoped that if it came to it, she would know how to handle it. She knew glaciers had swallowed up some of the best mountaineers.

Even if someone had been climbing mountains for forty years, they could miss a gaping crevasse and plummet two hundred feet to a rocky floor, a jagged ice cavern, or frigid water that would freeze your blood within seconds. *Why am I doing this?* she wondered, shivering.

"I'm so beat," Greg huffed and sat down next to Quinn, immediately digging into his food. He nodded over to her, "Thanks."

"No problem." She gave him a tired smile. Hours of bushwhacking with four thousand feet of elevation gain didn't make for the most relaxing stroll through the hills. Still, their most daunting challenge lay ahead. There were many reasons to visit the Southern Pickett Range. It was remote, beautiful, isolated, and primordial.

As always, Greg wanted to climb something no one else had ever finished. Tomorrow they would attempt a 5.12c variant of the north face on Mt. Terror.

The climb consisted of twelve rope-length sections, or pitches, on a mixed granite-and-ice wall. Most of the climbs on the line were rated 5.9–5.10b—moderate ratings that Quinn felt comfortable climbing. Greg had unearthed an archive written by climbers in the eighties who had tried the more difficult route and been forced to bail. Their variation had yet to be completed, and Greg was hoping to bag his debut first ascent. The two of them had spent many late nights reading maps, planning routes and hauls, and puzzling over all possible exit strategies in case of emergency. They had drilled on the lower slopes of Mt. Rainier, and they'd put in extra conditioning time for the climb over the past couple of months.

Greg's eyes narrowed as he studied the darkness around them. "You see anyone else on the way up here?" She hadn't, but then again, she'd mostly been thinking of how badly she wanted to drop her pack and get off her feet.

"I don't think so, why?" Quinn took a beer and kicked off her boots to warm her feet by the fire.

He shrugged. "When I was standing over by the glacier, I thought I saw someone."

"Climbers?"

Another shrug, one of Greg's signature moves. "It was weird. I thought I saw someone standing way out on the other side, wearing a red coat. Blinked, and they were gone."

"You hallucinating up here? I thought you were a mountaineer." With a wool-clad foot, she kicked a small rock at him playfully.

"Probably just trippin'." He looked back out to the glacier, casting a shimmering column of light over the dark lurking ice with his headlamp.

"Maybe someone's coat blew away on a previous trip like our tent almost did?" she joked, raising an eyebrow.

He chuckled and took the final scoop of his nightly rations. Then he sloshed some hot water into the bowl to rinse it out before placing it next to the fire. "I'm crashing. We've got an early start." He kissed her and turned for the tent.

She caught Greg's hand and gave it a quick kiss in return. "I'll be in soon," she said.

She sat alone for another thirty minutes, enjoying the silence that settled over the evening. The rustling sound of Greg reorganizing the tent finally subsided. *It's never quite right for him*, she mused. After sucking down the rest of her beer, she began to loll in her seat. Quinn left the fire smoldering since they were completely surrounded by rocky terrain and snow, and they would want warm embers in the morning. She retired to the tent, crawling as quietly as she could into the crinkling sleeping bag next to Greg.

What felt like two hours passed, and she was still tossing and turning. The bitter night air clung to her face, crisp and light but irritating like the tickle of a frigid feather. Quinn tucked her head into her sleeping bag, willing herself to sleep but there was nothing for it. Frustrated, she grabbed her headlamp, slid on her boots, and unzipped the tent door. Turning on the lamp, she stepped outside and over to the fire pit, where a few bold embers were still valiantly fighting for life.

The entire planet seemed eerily silent. It was the sort of silence one could only find when well and truly away from most other life. The mountains could be one of those places, yet she still felt the forest below should be alive with the odd bird, nocturnal rodent, or stalking predator. She heard absolutely nothing. The world was asleep but for her. As Quinn looked up the snowy slope again, she fixated on Terror Glacier, dreading the numerous hazards of her impending glacial travel.

Suddenly she felt an overwhelming sense of unease. It was not glacial anxiety—this was new. As if someone was watching her from across the valley. As a young woman, she had felt the sensation countless times. She turned around and shined her headlight into the black pines.

They towered—rooted, ancient, unconcerned. Quinn listened intently; she thought she could hear the telltale crunching of feet on snow. The steps were light and swift, like someone striding on bare feet.

The crunching stopped, returning the forest to silence. Then she heard it. The voice of a middle-aged man, scared but not panicked. His voice trembled slightly as he said, "Hello?"

Quinn froze. When she dared to swing her headlight to where she thought the voice came from, nobody was there. Only the trees, and they said nothing. She walked backward slowly, away from the dark looming forest as quietly as possible.

"Hello?" the voice asked, in exactly the same tone.

She kicked the side of the tent and hissed, "Greg, I hear a voice. Get up." Greg mumbled indistinctly. She kicked his leg through the nylon. The tent door unzipped forcefully.

"What the hell, babe? We gotta be up in, like, three hours," he seethed.

Quinn bent down quickly, putting a finger to her lips. He became serious. She cocked her head, listening harder. "I heard it. The—"

"Hello?" the voice asked again, much closer this time. It sounded no more than twenty feet away. The inflection was the same. From tone to timbre, it was tinged with some unnatural distortion, as if transmitted through the static of a radio. Greg's eyes widened. He began fumbling through his pack until he pulled out a large canister of bear spray. Shining her light into the woods again, she saw a quick blur of movement as something on the edge of the clearing darted out of her headlamp's beam.

Steadily, slowly, she crept around the tent and grabbed her ice axe as Greg stumbled out of his sleeping bag, bear spray in hand, headlamp clicked on.

"Someone's out there," Quinn said. He nodded and squeezed her shoulder reassuringly.

The two stood, moving their headlamps around, neither daring to leave the small circle of their campsite. The beams swept and searched, like a helicopter searching city streets for a car on the run. Their nervous breathing puffed into the air in small, quick whiffs. After what seemed an immeasurable amount of time, they ducked back into their tent and huddled together against the cold. Try as they did, neither slept a wink.

ELLIE

Ellie Jensen's truck radio crackled with feedback as dispatch continued to hail her, despite the fact that she'd told them three times she'd have no reception for the next day or so. She cranked her radio dial to zero with a callused forefinger to end its persistent crackling. *It's the damn off season. Get your shit together, people.* She knew it was wishful thinking, but she went ahead and thought it anyway. It *had* been a shit season so far, no denying.

She had always loved training qualified volunteers in the art of deep wilderness rescue, and leading search-and-rescue parties into the backwoods. Though mostly she babysat and trained youths on the basics of wilderness navigation. Lately, it had been different.

The first year, Ellie had been energized by their enthusiasm toward a fresh experience. Back then, it was easy to believe that people had respect for nature, that they had the best intentions for her precious forests, rivers, and crags. She wished she could still believe that but some days it was tough. This year had been harder than ever.

For some people, nature really did bring out their best qualities; it certainly did so for Ellie. For just as many, it brought out the disrespect, the hubris, the utter idiocy inherent in humankind—an idiocy that stood out starkest against the backdrop of the Washington Wilds. Professionals could post signs, give lectures, share videos on social media, and provide live weather feeds, but there would always be at least one person who translated 'bad conditions' into 'a mountain to myself.'

Those were the ones Ellie and her team excavated from avalanche zones. Tragic deaths and the scenes they left behind were not the worst of Ellie's work, as most people assumed.

Back when she was starting in search and rescue, deaths hit Ellie hard. Her first corpse with SAR had been a twenty-two-year-old woman who had drowned. Ellie had seen the girl in a hiking class; now she'd been regurgitated by the Sauk River—a bloated, pale-green body on the sandy, pebbled beach. Ellie had vomited right on a fellow volunteer's khakis. When she informed her first set of parents, she'd cried along with them over the loss of their son, a man she'd never known. She sought out a therapist for that one. Even after Baghdad she hadn't hired a counselor, and she'd seen many people die there. For some reason, the SAR deaths had been much worse.

After many deaths caused by inexperience, lack of preparation, and disrespect for nature, Ellie had become somewhat numb, much to her own frustration. Now, when she had to deliver the worst news parents, siblings, fiancés, and friends could ever hear, she did them all the same. Her words were rote knowledge—textbook, expected, and emotionless like a drive-thru employee asking, "Small, medium, or large?" However, today Ellie was forced to remember how it felt in the beginning. If she were to find Greg dead up in the mountains... She refused to even consider it.

Ellie shook off the thought and pressed a little harder on the gas. Despite the dangerous nature of these mountainous backroads, she could probably drive most of them with her eyes closed. In fact, one of her sinister joys in life was watching new recruits white-knuckle the 'oh shit' handles when she drove, taking the hairpin turns at thirty-five on gravel.

Right now, she was heading out to one of her favorite old stomping grounds, the Southern Pickets. It was a gorgeous little range; remote enough to keep out all the cool rollers and kids, but navigable enough that anyone with a sack and the ability to use a compass could find it.

She preferred the places that people went if they were serious over the ones people went to pretend they liked the outdoors. If you hiked out to the Pickets in your brand-new hiking pants and shiny boots, they'd be broken-in pants and scuffed, muddy boots by the end of the trip. For Ellie, that's what made it a place worth going.

Most years, there were few accidents in the Pickets, hardly anyone hiked them at all. The only ones interested in hiking that deep were climbers. *Climbers like Greg, and it's been a weird-ass year out here.*

Ellie assumed the recent spike in disappearances came with the growing popularity of the sport. The approach seemed simple enough when casual day hikers and climbers accustomed to places like Frenchman Coulee and Exit 38 arrived in the paved parking lot. As soon as the nicely manicured trail turned into one with bushwhacking and class-four scrambling, it became remarkably easy for the inexperienced to become lost. She used to find it fascinating and depressing how little respect people had for the dangers of the mountains.

Just then, she was snaking her Toyota around a devious S-bend that claimed at least two vehicles and their drivers every year. The fastest anyone had ever flown off it was sixty mph.

Even she slowed down to fifteen for that cock sucker. She remembered her younger, more optimistic self who'd theorized that it was one part hubris and two parts thrill that sent people hurtling off cliff faces.

* * *

"What's the scariest animal in the mountains?" asked twenty-two-year-old Ellie from the beanbag seat on her college dorm floor. She faced the webcam with determination, having finally stumbled upon what a bottle of red wine had convinced her was a fantastic allegory.

Through the digital window, live on Skype from Bellingham, was her boyfriend, Roger Nelson. "Humans," he answered without a second's hesitation, "they can't even help being dangerous to themselves. Isn't that the whole point of this conversation?"

"No, no... I mean, well, yeah, but not counting humans."

"Bears?" Roger asked, this time with a glimmer of contemplation. He had clearly failed to realize the fantasticalness of Ellie's forthcoming metaphor, so she enlightened him.

"EHN! Wrong!" she shrieked in her best imitation of a gameshow buzzer. Roger covered his ears with both hands.

"Okay, a moose," he said, seemingly certain enough of his answer to uncover his ears. Ellie assumed he, like many people, had heard moose killed lots of people. Also, like most people, he had not bothered to do any research.

"EHN! Wrong again!" she said. "Most moose-murdered women and men are driving when it happens, with the unfortunate moose just standing on the highway being god-damned huge." After a contemplative gaze toward the ceiling and a healthy swig of wine, Ellie continued, "They're the scapegoats of the natural world."

Before she finished speaking, Roger was shaking his head. "No, no, no. First of all, I'd say wolves are the scapegoats of the natural world. They get the worst rap ever. They hardly kill anyone," he huffed, raising himself up into what Ellie called his 'listen here' pose as he gained some traction with his argument. "You asked a subjective question, and I gave a statistically sound and personalized answer. A horny moose is one of the nastiest bastards on the planet, and a female with calves..." He left the sentence unfinished as if unable to express the magnitude of nasty that a calf-laden female moose embodied.

"No. See... see, that's my whole point," she said, slightly slurring her words.

"Ah, yeah. I was wondering if we'd ever get to that," he snarked.

Ellie plowed on, refusing to smile, but only just. Their arguments always had the best intentions. "The scariest animal in the mountains is the one you don't see," she said. "Think about it. Nobody watches a video on skydiving and buys a parachute the next day to go jumping off a cliff. They pay twelve thousand bucks to take a class and go up in a plane with a guide. Skydiving is like a moose. The danger is obvious and in your face. You just know not to fuck with a moose. Or a bear, for that matter. The mountains are more dangerous than skydiving, and they kill more people because they're like a cougar." She took what began as a sip but became a hearty swallow, which then warranted a refill of the wine glass.

"That was the answer, by the way. A cougar is the scariest animal in the mountains." Gulp, gulp, sigh, and wipe that upper lip—goodbye white pajama sleeves.

Roger mimed writing notes in an imaginary notebook, a look of studious concentration on his face. "Will this be on the test?" he asked.

"Yes, and so will my fantastic-ass metaphor, if you'd shut the hell up," she said, maintaining her stern facade.

Roger shut the hell up.

"The mountains kill you patiently. Most people die of hypothermia and exposure 'cause they aren't careful enough to stay dry, but they don't even think about it 'til they start to shiver, and by then, it's already a good way along. Cougars are like hypothermia. They will stalk you for ten miles and never make a move. You'll never know a cougar is there until it's too late." She raised her wine glass in a triumphant flourish. "It's all hubris. People don't even consider things dangerous or challenging until it's right in front of them."

* * *

Looking back on that night, everything had seemed so promising. They had continued to argue playfully for the rest of the night. But the next morning, she'd started boot camp and her military journey, which had spelled death for their relationship.

Over the past three years of working SAR, her belief that hubris was a climber's downfall solidified. Most of her job amounted to tracking down idiots who had tried to follow a phone app into the woods.

Phones die or get damaged, and *bang*, someone's hopelessly lost. An astonishing number of people in the woods not only couldn't read a topographical map or compass but didn't even bring them along.

Those damn people read 'Into the Wild' and decide they want to be Chris McCandless, she thought, *without bothering to remember how the whole adventuring-blindly-into-the-wild thing worked out for him.* She shook the thought from her head. *That's not Greg. I trained him. He knows what he's doing.*

Dust billowed up behind the tires of her Toyota 4Runner as she climbed higher into the densely wooded foothills of the North Cascades. The road was an overgrown hallway of thorny blackberry tangles, towering cedars, and firs interspersed with slabby granite crags. As Ellie pulled into the campground, she saw four vehicles parked there. One was a green Ford Ranger with the license plate SEND513. She eyed it suspiciously and jotted it down in her notepad: *Greg's vehicle at the trailhead, mud on tires is dry.*

A group of campers was packing up their tents and camping chairs, so she approached them. The fact that she was holding a manila folder, along with her attire of cargo khakis, black button-up shirt, and tightly bound bun of otherwise rebellious brown curls, seemed to culminate into an image of law enforcement to the young campers. As she neared, they hurriedly hid what looked like a small plastic bong underneath one of their packs.

Ellie's sharp brown eyes fixed on them, ignoring the paraphernalia. Following this completely conspicuous concealment, they adopted a matching demeanor of suburban church-goers. *Who could suspect a gosh-darn thing?*

"Hey, guys," Ellie said, not entirely unlike an officer of the law would have. "I'm looking for some friends of mine. I think they came in that green Ranger." She pulled a picture of Greg from her folder. "Seen him?"

The young blonde exchanged looks with a brunette girl who looked at the teenage boy next to her. He was obviously her boyfriend as his hand was blatantly caressing her inner thigh. *Forgot to shut that circuit down for the 'Church Boy' act.* The lovebirds gave a joint apathetic shrug. Likely they'd seen little but the inside of a tent since they'd drunkenly stumbled into that nylon sex palace last night. *Oh, to be young again.* Pretty Brunette and Boy Toy went back to packing. The blonde, however, walked over. Ellie wiggled the picture of Greg. In it, he was smiling, dressed in hiking clothes, and leaning against a tree. The girl looked at the picture but shook her head.

"Sorry," she said, avoiding Ellie's eyes, "I didn't see anyone. That pickup was here before we showed up. We were just here one night."

"That's what I figured." Ellie hesitated. Pretty Blonde was staring at her with what looked like genuine concern. "Did you see anything you'd like to tell me about?" Ellie asked in a lowered, more confidential tone. The girl looked nervous.

"I... are we in trouble?" she asked, wringing her hands.

"I'm not the cops. I don't care if you're drinking beer or smoking that bong or banging each other out here." Ellie smiled, and the girl flushed furiously. Her friends giggled, Pretty Brunette hiding her face behind Boy Toy's shoulder.

"I'm Ellie," she said, holding out her hand. "I like sex and booze too. Everyone does." The girl's face blushed a deeper red, which Ellie would have bet was impossible. All the same, the girl shook her hand.

"I'm Grace." She looked down at her shoes, then back up to Ellie. "Thanks."

"You don't have to thank me. I didn't do anything. Now, Grace, is there anything you can do to help me find this guy? He was out here rock climbing, and I'm worried he might have gotten hurt."

Grace took her time considering her reply. She looked like she was trying to recall a foggy memory of something that had occurred in the midst of a drunken ride down lovers' lane as the dreaded third wheel. Behind her, the other two teens were extracting the bong. After a brief, hushed argument, Boy Toy seemed to win because Pretty Brunette took a massive bong rip. *Oh, yeah, these two are gonna make some dumbass kids.*

"I think I heard someone, but it was really late. It sounded like someone was in the trees. But, like, way high up." Grace shrugged. "I figured I just imagined it. I was sorta drunk," the young blonde admitted with a shy smile.

"What did they say?"

"Just hello." Grace looked toward the trailhead. "Sounded like it came from really high up there, almost like… I don't know. No one else came by, and the only other vehicle was your friend's. Maybe it was your friend. But when I called out, nobody answered. I might have just imagined it. I haven't gotten drunk many times."

Boy Toy, who had clearly been eavesdropping as he pretended to pack up his tent, perked up. "I thought you said you got drunk all the time, Grace?"

"So, you *were* drunk after one beer?" Her friend laughed, puffing out a bit of residual smoke. The boyfriend chuckled along, causing Grace to look at her shoes again.

Ellie lightly put a hand on her shoulder. "Most boys suck at his age. Don't worry, they get better." She pondered that before amending, "Plenty of them do, anyways. You just gotta find the right one."

With a hopeful nod, Grace turned back to her friends. Halfway there, she stopped and turned back. "I hope you find your friend," she offered, with another shy smile.

"Thanks, Grace." Ellie pulled out a business card and handed it to the girl. "If you remember anything else, please let me know. I think my friend is in real trouble." Grace accepted the card and retreated to her camping chair. As Ellie approached the trailhead, she heard the boy arguing behind her.

"Great job, narc. Got the cop's card and everything."

"She's a mountain guide, stupid. She's looking for her friend."

"That's what a cop would say," her brunette friend chimed in, though not so concerned that she refrained from another hit.

Ellie shook her head. *At least these ones didn't go up any farther than the campground.* Ellie's instincts were as solid as glacier-carved granite. She could always tell when someone was seriously in trouble or just off trail. She had a bad feeling about Greg. Her instincts told her time was short.

QUINN

Nearing the edge of Terror Glacier, Quinn stared straight ahead as the seemingly flat and harmless-looking plain of snow transformed into a landscape of ice structures, cracks, and fissures. Now that she was standing before it, she remembered exactly why she had wanted to refuse Greg's invite in the first place. He'd said there was lots to do in the Pickets. They could hike to a glacial lake. "Just six miles from camp," he'd promised. They could do the West McMillan Spire. "Nice and easy," he'd sworn. And then, "We don't have to do the glacier if you don't want to," he'd vowed, "We'll just look at it and see how it shapes up." They'd done all those things, and a few more, and they'd been there for six days. A few days longer than they said they'd be out, and of course, Greg had not let anyone know. Not his parents. Not Ellie, who always looked out for him.

He was like that. Not selfish, necessarily, simply focused. His parents and Ellie would be worried, but he wasn't about to lose a day of climbing just to hike back for cell service. So, when they'd finished all their side projects and Greg still showed no signs of packing up camp, she'd realized it had always been a foregone conclusion: they were going to cross that glacier, and Greg was determined to try his climb. He'd never intended anything else.

"Yeah, I mean, there's one glacier to cross to get to Mt. Terror, but I can lead the way, and we'll mark our route with flags so we only have to do the hard bit once," he'd reassured her when she'd asked if the trip would include glacial travel.

Filled with anxiety and trepidation she eyed the glacier. "Greg, we've had this conversation before. After last time, I really don't feel comfortable with it."

"Quinn." He looked deeply into her eyes, giving her his most reassuring smile. "I have crossed the Terror a dozen times. It doesn't have as many crevasses as Mt. Baker. It's a well-documented fact. We can sit down with a map and go through the topo again. It won't be like last time."

"I know," she said, putting her hand on his after some consideration. The only thing she hated more than being afraid was feeling weak. "I guess it's part of the game."

"Really?" he asked. She shrugged in resignation, only slightly resentful. It was enough for Greg.

Moments later, when she was preparing to cross the field of ice canyons and caves hidden beneath an indeterminate depth of soft snow, she wished she had just said, *No, Greg. I will climb on any rock with you, I'll shit in plastic bags and hang on the side of a wall all day, but I am done with goddamn glaciers. I'd appreciate it if you respected that like you promised you would.* But she knew Greg's stoke made him blind to other people's concerns, even if those were justified. Quinn loved and hated that about him.

Greg pulled his face mask over his mouth and lowered his goggles as he tromped up to her. His cheeks arched in a way that told her he was giving her his reassuring smile again. "Ready?"

Quinn shrugged.

"Okay, just stay close and test the snow before you step. You'll be fine," he said, then crunched on out. She glanced back over her shoulder, surveying the area around their camp for any sign of movement. "If that person was going to hurt us, he would have already," Greg had said, all rational reassurance, dismissing her apprehension about the strange voice as easily as her fear for the glacier.

The rope at her waist went tight, prompting her focus forward. *I'm just nervous about the glacier. Everything's fine.* She forced herself to concentrate on the task at hand.

Greg prodded the snow with each step. Here and there, snow fell away into thin cracks, but they didn't encounter any huge crevasses like they had near Mt. Baker last year, when Quinn had fallen into one. Every fifteen feet, Greg would pull a long pink-flagged garden stake from the side pocket of his pack and jam it into the snow to mark the safe path.

They were over the glacier in no time. As Quinn's boots scraped solid rock, she breathed a sigh she'd been holding the entire morning. Greg, still leading the charge on the other end of their loose climbing rope, turned around and tossed her a quick thumbs up. She flipped one back and continued following him toward Mt. Terror.

Now safely on the other side, she felt better. Not good, but better. She truly had been looking forward to this climb, and she'd overcome a big personal hurdle.

She breathed again, deeper this time, inhaling the cold soothing freshness of the alpine air. Usually, that was enough to clear her head of worry and place her in a state of blissful meditation. Since it didn't seem to be working today, she chose to focus on Greg as he looked up the face of the mountain before them. His worship for the outdoors and his sport was inspiring, and she tried to draw from it. *He shares this part of his world with me. I need to be worthy of that.*

Try as she might, Quinn couldn't shake a sickening sense of dread. Instead of looking up as Greg was, toward their goal, she felt a constant urge to look back over her shoulder. She'd hoped the feeling would dissipate after the glacier, but the dread remained, making her feel like a rabbit under a sky of circling hawks. *Where the hell did that voice come from last night?* It was too late to mention it again. She'd crossed the glacier, her biggest hurdle of the day, and Greg was so utterly focused that he hadn't said a word to her since. He was already tying in and waiting for the all clear to start climbing. *Once we're up there, we'll be safe,* she assured herself.

"Alright, I got my figure eight, got my harness double backed, got all my gear. You good to go?" he asked.

"You're on belay," she said, showing him her Grigri device with the rope correctly oriented through it. A locking carabiner secured the Grigri to her belay loop. "Well, actually, you're not, but you will be," she chuckled. "I'm ready." He smiled and began his climb.

Quinn watched him ascend until the kink in her neck forced her to drop her gaze to the cliff face in front of her. She felt the slack, making sure to give Greg enough to continue without fighting her, but not so much that he'd take a huge fall if he lost his footing. Continuing to feed out rope dutifully, she periodically looked up to monitor his progress. She saw he had already reached the first belay ledge and was building an anchor.

"Safe!" He leaned back from the wall and put his full weight on his anchor system, which he'd placed above the ledge. "Off belay!"

"Off belay!" she shouted in confirmation, as she always did. She'd read too many stories of miscommunication leading to death in the mountains.

"Off belay!" he responded. She removed the rope from her Grigri. Not a moment later, the rope began whizzing up the wall as Greg hauled it up. She could see him flaking the rope into neat, even loops over his leg. Eventually, the rope tied to her harness went taut, jerking her lightly toward the wall. He continued to tug, nearly making her lose her balance.

"That's me!" she shouted. A moment of silence.

"ON BELAY!" he bellowed down, looking over his shoulder at her.

"Climbing!" she yelled back. He tossed her a thumbs up, and she began her ascent. She was excited and nervous, as always, but there was something else. *What the hell is up with me today? Maybe I'm just not in it right now.* She forced her foot to take a high step onto a slick, rime-covered ledge, and eased herself vertical.

ELLIE

Ellie turned off the forest service road as soon as she had a bar on her phone. She sighed and cranked her radio on. "Lynn, are you still around?" she inquired into her small receiver. It crackled for a few moments before coming to life.

"That you, Jensen?" Lynn's voice was assured, authoritative, and compassionate all at once, tempered as it was from the fires of two decades of dispatch duty.

"It's me." A smile cracked Ellie's stern visage, as always when she was talking to Lynn.

"Where you been all day?"

"Checking out the Goodell Creek campground."

"Anyone there?"

"A couple campers. Two vehicles. Have you heard anything back from missing persons?"

"Your missing climber?"

"Yeah."

"Nothing yet. They don't always let us know when things go right, though. Mostly just chew our asses when they don't. I'll check in tomorrow morning when they got someone around."

"Cool. Listen, Lynn, I'm gonna go up to the Pickets for the next couple days if y'all don't need me."

"Climbing?"

There was a pause between the two women, the crackling of the radio filling the silence.

"Need backup?" Lynn tried instead.

"Nah. Should be pretty routine."

"Be careful out there, Jensen. Been a weird year."

"Yeah, it has." They were simple words, but they were heavy. Lynn, Ellie, and many other experienced SAR members were growing concerned.

"Well," Lynn drawled out, "good luck. Call if you need us. Let me know when you get back, so I can get you on assignment."

"Yes, *Mom*."

"Don't forget to pack a lunch."

After clicking off her radio, Ellie cracked her window to let the sounds and smells of the alpine road flood her senses. Despite the beauty of the high mountain world, she couldn't muster a smile. She was filled with an anxiety that she couldn't quite place, one that had been growing throughout the year. Lynn's words rang in her head like the swirling wind in her pickup: *Been a weird year.*

Ellie had been in plenty of sketchy situations. She'd been in operation Desert Storm, snowed into a cave for three days, washed down the Skagit rapids for two miles, treed by a pissed-off brown bear, and stalked by a cougar. She'd even been stalked by a couple dumbass men from a seedy bar in Seattle, but her black belt in jujitsu had helped her sort them out. Although she was neither unfamiliar with nor afraid of danger, she did get nervous when encountering the inexplicable.

Explanation was her life, her profession. Danger was always present in nature, but it could be explained, trained, and prepared for. She treated rescues just the same.

She'd been on hundreds of SAR calls and had had less than five complete disappearances in her entire career, until this past season. There was always a discernible explanation, something to tell the families and friends, lawyers and cops.

This season, despite it being spring, the mountains seemed dead as December. The forest was quiet, as if even the plants were holding their breath. The first climber who'd been lost over the last year might have faded from her memory as another victim to the Terror Glacier. The crevasses were getting worse every year, and even experienced mountaineers following established routes could end up falling into one. Crevasses could open up to a five-hundred-foot drop, ending in a freezing cold lake. A complete disappearance there was easily explained.

Not a month later, though, three day hikers had gone missing, and a couple weeks after that, two kayakers. Unlike the first, those occurrences had no explanation. In Ellie's experience, that meant something out of the ordinary was occurring, possibly something human. *The most dangerous animal in the mountains. No question.*

* * *

Dinner with Roger and his wife, Rachel, had felt off. It had been one of those nights where everything seemed forced, robotic, obligatory. Ellie had not been uncomfortable with Roger since their break up twenty-five years ago. Feeling that way now didn't sit right with her. She could sense Roger's low energy. As if he wasn't present. He was the sort of man who treated every interaction like it was the only conversation occurring in the universe. That Friday night he hadn't even seemed to be on the same planet, but he and Rachel went through the motions, making small talk, joking and laughing, then leaving on an obviously pre-established pretense at 9:30 p.m. *What a weird fuckin' night.*

By then, Ellie had been wondering why her friends had come over at all. She had stayed up long after they left, drinking alone, wondering if Roger and Rachel were fighting on her account. It was a strange thought but she couldn't shake the vibe that she was being excluded, left out of some big, overarching problem which perforated their usual connectivity. All the easy, synchronistic joys and humors they usually shared had bled out between those figurative holes. It had been years since she'd felt this sort of tension between her and Rachel.

When Rachel and Roger had started dating, his previous relationship and friendship with Ellie had been a problem for Rachel. Now, with all issues of jealousy firmly in the past, Ellie had thought she would no longer have to worry about dredging up that discussion with either of them. After that dinner, and three-fourths of a bottle of Jameson, she had begun to wonder if that wasn't exactly what she needed to do. Ellie resolved to head over to the Nelson family home in the morning so she could catch Roger. That was how Ellie Jensen handled awkward situations. She confronted them, head on.

Ellie pulled into the Nelsons' driveway just in time to catch her unsuspecting friend on his way out the door. Roger threw her a forced smile and exaggerated wave as he made his way over to her car.

"Hey, Ell. Did I leave something at your place last night?"

"Nah, I just wanted to talk to you," she said, concern plain in her voice. Still, Roger attempted to keep up his pleasant facade.

"Sure, what's on your mind?"

"What's on yours? Something's up, and that's what I'm worried about."

He looked as if he might dodge the issue but reconsidered. When he seemed to have decided to be honest with her, his countenance melted away, revealing a version of her best friend she barely recognized. Tears welled in the corners of his eyes as he said, "Alright, then. Why don't you come in?" Roger turned quickly and headed back toward his house.

She took her eyes off him and noticed that Rachel's car was gone; not unusual for a Saturday morning since she was a nurse at the St. Joseph's Hospital. Greg, Roger's son, drove a weathered, old Ford Ranger. It was gone too. *With what I'm about to bring up, that's probably for the best,* she reflected. She swung around Roger's sedan and backed into Rachel's usual spot. *He wouldn't talk about shit if anyone else was around.*

Roger had always kept his thoughts closely guarded. Ellie did too. At this point in their lives, though, they really had no choice but to trust each other. They had far too many shared memories and drunken heart-to-hearts for anything else.

"Sorry about the mess," Roger said over his shoulder, leaving the door ajar. "Rachel and I have hardly slept the last couple of days."

Rachel usually had the place cleaner than the hospital. There, she couldn't enforce her iron-clad 'shoes off in the house' rule. But in the Nelson home were meticulously mopped floors, glistening counters, neatly closed doors, and precisely placed pillows on the couch and loveseat. Sometimes Ellie even felt guilty for moving them to sit.

As Ellie entered now, she saw the love seat and its pillow buried in a pile of unfolded laundry. Paperwork and mail were strewn across the table in the dining room, and two open laptops were on the couch and the coffee table. The large glass door adjoining the dining room and kitchen generally allowed adequate lighting for the whole living room, but the blinds were drawn shut. A gloomy, yellowish light cast a feeling of sickness over the disheveled house. Whatever Roger was going through, Rachel was too. In addition to the obvious signs, Ellie felt like the house was missing a vital component of its soul. Like part of the abstract foundation had rotted away, rendering it cracked and uneven.

"Coffee?" Roger offered as he brushed a pile of laundry onto the floor to clear a space for her to sit.

"Sure, thanks," she replied, trying to put the scene together to form some logical conclusion. Roger emerged from the kitchen and handed her a steaming mug. She took a precautionary sip as he sunk into what had clearly become a habitual depression in the cushion, that absorbed him like a sponge soaking up a spill. He let out a deep sigh and started to fill her in. Tears that could no longer be held back spilled out.

"It's, uh... it's Greg," he choked, the words struggling their way through his quivering vocal cords. "We think he might be missing." Despite the maelstrom of emotions, his last sentence rang hollow, as if he didn't believe it.

Ellie looked down, noticing the back-and-forth paths on Rachel's usually glossy hardwood, and noted Roger was still wearing his shoes. For a few long moments, she had nothing to say.

"Fuck," she finally managed, her voice cracking slightly. "I'm... I mean, what's going on?"

"Kid's a maniac. You know that," Roger said, tears streaming down his face freely. "Only a matter of time, I guess."

"Where's he climbing?" she asked with a pang of guilt.

"The Pickets. He texted me early last week to let me know, but he was supposed to be back two days ago. Greg has been late before but never more than a day."

The Pickets? As soon as Greg had expressed interest in what she did, Ellie had begun taking him hiking and eventually on climbing trips. Greg knew the Pickets well and was probably just taking a few extra days to enjoy them. She considered saying this to Roger but figured it would be empty consolation.

"I know he's been out there plenty, but anyone can get turned around. It's still cold up there. I mean, there's snow on the goddamn mountains. They say that..." Roger's voice trailed off.

"Who's he out there with?"

"His girlfriend, Quinn. You met her before, I think."

"Yeah, a couple times. She's a good kid."

He nodded absently. "Maybe one of them just had a fall, and it's taking them longer to get back. Who knows?" He shrugged.

"Hey," she said, "we don't know shit right now." Roger stared into his mug so hard it seemed he was trying to discern the backstory of the beans that had brewed it. "Dude?" She stood and walked over to the couch, moved the laptop, and sat next to him. "Why didn't you tell me?"

He looked at her with a guilty expression. "I wanted to tell you last night, but Rachel didn't want me to."

"Why the hell not?"

"She wants to have faith in him. He is an adult," he defended. Ellie opened her mouth, but shut it again and let him continue. "Until a couple days ago, it wasn't that out of the ordinary. If we called the cops or you every time we were worried about him, he'd disown us." Ellie imagined having a mountaineer for a son would be a grueling reality for some parents, probably like having a daughter in the Marines. *Sorry, Pops.*

"Okay. I can understand that. If you want, I can head out there and check up on him."

"I don't wanna put you out."

She knew refusing help was a staple of his personality. "Fuck that, man." She stood and stalked toward the door.

"You have some extra gear? I should come with you."

"You ain't a mountaineer, Rog. You'll slow me down."

"He's my son."

She put a firm hand on his shoulder, her grip assuring but final. "I know the area. You'll hear from me by next weekend. And I'll have Greg safe and sound. You hear me?"

"Thanks, Ellie," he said. "I just have a terrible feeling this time. I can't explain it. Is there anything I can do to help?"

"Take care of yourself, eat something. Take care of Rachel too. I'll be in touch."

She drove away from Roger's house, feeling responsible for the family's plight. She had taken Greg to the Pickets many times. If he had been two days late by his parents reckoning, then he'd likely been up there six days more than he planned, assuming he had taken Ellie's advice: "Always give yourself a four-day grace period on a long expedition since people who don't climb rarely understand the dangers of a committed descent." If he was six days late, then he might well be dead in a crevasse with her other vanished climbers. He might be on his way to becoming another one of Ellie's rapidly growing list of unexplained disappearances. She didn't want to consider that.

GREG

Greg flaked the rope into a messy pile on the large shelf from which he'd belayed Quinn. The monotonous movement of the rope through his fingers relaxed him as he studied the crack system to the small ledge. That crack marked the end of the next section of the climb. Two pitches farther up loomed an overhanging chimney. After that, he'd have to tackle the off-width crack and a run-out section of slab: the infamous eighth pitch. If he could pull this eighth pitch off, the rest of the climb would be as easy as cracking a cold beer back at base camp. He certainly didn't relish the prospect of falling off, but he knew every gut-wrenching, back-tweaking, bowel-shifting fall would be entirely worth it.

Beside him, Quinn was selecting the gear he would need and clipping it onto his harness. Lost in their thoughts and preparations, they worked in silence. Despite the nervous energy crackling down his spine and swirling through his stomach, there was nowhere Greg would rather be. He put his hands on the face, preparing to climb, testing his holds and footing.

"Hey, lemme check you before you start," Quinn said, anxiousness in her voice.

He sighed and dropped back onto the shelf. They'd checked their gear at every pitch, as she always insisted. Nothing had changed in terms of Greg's climbing knot or harness, and he hadn't taken any falls today.

He quickly peeked at Quinn's belay, saw it was configured correctly, and turned back to the rock. She tugged on the rope, turning him toward her so she could see his setup.

It's not enough to see it, you gotta recite it out loud, he thought sarcastically. "Hole smaller than my fist, through my two hard points, two, four, six, eight strands, and my Yosemite finish." He listed each integral aspect of his protective knot, then displayed it irritably to Quinn. She didn't look impressed. *Wastin' daylight,* he thought.

"You can make fun of me if you want. I'm always gonna check your gear 'cause if it's wrong, you'll die." She gave him her 'and that's a fact' look. He knew not to argue, but he wasn't about to stay on this ledge. He turned and put his hands and feet back on the wall.

"On belay?" he asked flatly.

"Yeah, you're on belay." Quinn rang her carabiner to show that it was locked. He started climbing, leaving the argument to simmer tensely beneath him.

When he scaled up ten feet, he balanced himself on the precarious holds that marked his placement stance and wedged a .5 cam into the small notch at the base of the crack system. He quickly snagged the rope that hung limp from his harness, clipped it into his first piece of protection, and gave it a sharp tug to test its stability. Then he continued on his route. He tried not to think about Quinn, glaring up at him from her ledge. *Why's she even up here if she's scared?* She was so damn anxious sometimes. It wore him out. *How am I supposed to focus when she's like that?*

He climbed to the first belay ledge with little difficulty. After he secured himself, he established a solid anchor from which he could bring his partner up.

Quinn took much longer to complete the pitch, but eventually she hauled herself onto the ledge next to him. She was breathing heavily as she clipped her PAS—personal anchor system—into his anchor. She took a few moments to catch her breath, then stood up and returned to the standard routine of beginning the next pitch. Flake rope, organize gear, set up a belay.

As much as he loved actively climbing, ledge time had always been one of Greg's favorite parts of the experience. Just he and a trusted climbing partner so high above the world that it might have been another planet. The wind all one could hear. The swirling snow and clouds, the epic sweeping landscapes that were all he could or would ever need to see. The clean air and cold bite of the wind was part of his soul. Every time Greg was back on the ground, he knew the mountains were there, looming in the distance, a pathway to the heavens. They were calling for him to return.

When Greg looked down, he didn't see a drop to certain death. He saw all the majesty of the Cascades, the rolling plains, the dense woodlands, and the stormy oceans. The ability to view the earth from a ledge was a gift that few ever enjoyed. Greg wished Quinn could relish it the way he did, wished she could see the beauty without the filter of fear. *It's not her fault she's afraid.* He looked at his partner, feeling guilty but refusing to admit it.

Suddenly she peered up at him. "I'm not gonna apologize for being safe, and I don't think it's fair for you to be mad about it," she said, sounding more hurt than angry. Greg just turned his head and stared up the climb. They worked in silence for a moment.

Sucking in a breath, considering how to reply, he glanced at her. "You're right. I'm just focused. I want to get this finished before dark."

She nodded, clipping the last of the gear on his harness. "Yeah."

Greg's heart lurched with guilt. He put a hand on Quinn's shoulder. "Thanks, Quinn."

"What?"

He didn't know what to say, so he said, "I love you." Her face remained hard, but when he turned back to the wall, she rubbed the back of his calf reassuringly. He showed her his knot, this time in a non-mocking way.

"Everything looking good, partner?" he asked.

"Looks good."

"Okay. Climbing?"

"Climb on."

Greg climbed on. *Gotta pick your battles.* He'd learned that from his parents.

The initial nervousness which always quarreled with his stoke at the start of a climb began to fade. The excitement receded too, but not as much. It was less of a fading and more a merging of the two emotions. When he climbed enough that it was safer to go up than to descend, the focus invigorated him. His entire universe became wind and rock and breath and balance. All he had to do was move through it. *I'm ascendin' this shit today.*

He scrambled the next pitch, and Quinn followed, making good time. Greg was glad to see she was feeling more comfortable. She always did when he was patient and supportive. Patience was not Greg's strongest attribute. He'd been taught how to climb by his no-nonsense 'rub some dirt in it' Aunt Ellie. Such mantras were not Quinn's notion of support, and he was working on that. Watching her confidently climb, the wind whipping her hair around her face as she pulled over icy jugs and balanced on razor-thin crimps with determination, he knew she was worth the effort.

"Alright!" She clapped his back and started looting his gear loops. "My lead?"

"You got this one?"

"I got it." She counted the pitches ahead and smirked at him. "You trying to time this so that I have to climb that crux first?"

"Uh huh, talk that shit." He laughed. "I was hoping you'd be up for leading the next two so I can rest up to tackle that crack. Cool?" Her smile broadened, and she nodded. Safety accounted for, Quinn began leading pitch six.

ELLIE

Ellie blazed up the switchbacks and overgrown backpacking trails with a fervor bordering on feverish. Roger had always teased her that if she just altered her gait a bit, she'd be running, not hiking. That day, her pace and stride were even longer and faster, and she planned to keep it up. Despite the urgency of her task and her determination, she was tired, depleted, and more nervous than she'd felt since her time with the Jarheads when people had been actively shooting at her. Something was definitely off.

The serene mountain air whipping gently though the trees morphed in her mind into the Iraqi desert's ever-present wind that blew sand and debris across the shattered concrete of war-torn streets. The sweet smells of the North Cascades, usually smells of profound relaxation and contentment for her, now felt intrusive. Rather than refresh, they repelled, like the acrid reek which hung over corpses, abandoned homes, and obliterated history. Nothing took flight. Not a crow cawed, no squirrel chittered. Flowers bloomed brilliantly, but no bees were buzzing around. It was as if the forest was a scene in a movie that had been paused. All she heard was her irritatingly heaving breaths and her clomping hikers.

This is nothing new. Everything will be in its place. Ellie huffed, dropped her pack to the dirt, and dug out her water bottle. She chugged the lukewarm water, readjusted her sweat-drenched shirt, returned the bottle to her pack, and was just about to sling the pack back over her shoulders when she noticed something on the forest soil. She knelt in the brush about ten feet off the trail, looking intently at the ground. *Tell yourself it's normal all you want, but look around. The woods are telling you something.*

She ducked into the underbrush and spotted a small red dot of blood beaded on a leaf. *Recon, my favorite,* she thought as she traced the faint blood trail through the dense underbrush. Ellie plowed through waist-high ferns, blackberry thorns, and low-hanging cedar branches until she came to a small patch of grass that was flattened and browning in a perfect circle. It looked like something large had bedded down here. The symmetry of the dead grass stood out starkly against its lush surroundings, as did the larger amount of blood present. She wouldn't call it a pool, but it was the beginning of a *real* blood trail leading into the woods ahead.

Ellie stood, pale-faced, and took a deep breath before she continued to follow the crimson path. She absentmindedly put a hand on the .44 Magnum she always carried when in the mountains. As she continued, she discovered an alarming amount of blood. *If this is human blood, that's a dead human.* She stopped and plucked something from the brush. It was a thick tuft of coarse black hair, coated in the sticky, red fluid. She held it up to get a better look in the sunlight.

"Black bear." It didn't take long before she reached the carcass of the beast. As soon as she spotted the corpse, she immediately recoiled and looked away. Ellie rarely got squeamish. She'd seen climbers' bodies after thousand-foot falls, fellow soldiers blown up by a landmine, and children frozen to death. The sight of this was terrible, brutal, and savage. The smell even worse. What made Ellie flinch, though, was the pure lack of nature in the killing. It was a terrible desecration of the natural world, and it was horrifically intentional.

A large black bear sow was impaled on a tree, which, judging by the splintered nature of the break, looked like it had been split by hand, despite the fact that it was a foot in diameter. The jagged edge of the tree jutted from the top of the bear's neck, forcing its head to the side at a grotesque angle like a macabre meat skewer. The bear had been skinned, making it look like a creature from an alien world. Its tongue lolled loosely from its mouth; intestines hung from within the flaps of its turned-out torso. From their mother's intestines, two young cubs hung, skinned and disemboweled. The smaller intestines hung to the ground and formed a strange circular symbol. The corpses seemed relatively fresh.

The strangest thing was not the symbol with large pools of blood completing a pattern in its center. The strangest thing was not even the circular flattened, dead grass. The strangest thing was that, despite three fresh corpses with their flesh turned, no scavengers were picking a meal from the decaying flesh. As if this was a neighborhood of such profound evil even the fly parents wouldn't raise their little maggots here.

At that moment, Ellie would have welcomed any sound. A mosquito, a buzzing swarm of flies, or even the roar of a large predator to claim easy prey or protect its kill. But all she could hear was her heart pounding in her chest. Ellie Jensen, the bold, courageous, and headstrong-to-a-fault woman stood pale against the greenery. That damnable, cloying silence clung to the forest like the sweaty shirt on her back. Unlike the shirt, she couldn't peel the quiet from the woods. It was part of the forest now.

QUINN

As soon as she weighted her first foothold, her leg began to quiver. *Fuck, Quinn. You know how to climb. Focus on the climb,* she reminded herself. After following Greg for four rope lengths, it was always difficult to take the sharp end of the rope. If she fell, she'd fall twice as far as her nearest protection, making every step a calculated risk and falling—or even resting off the wall—less of an option. She loved climbing, but it was easier to love it when she wasn't terrified of every step she took. Greg would tell her that falling was just part of the game. Quinn knew that. It still sucked.

With every ounce of mental fortification she could muster, she resisted the urge to look down. The yawning void pulled at her like a million grasping hands, making her all too aware of gravity's presence, only being held at bay by metal carabiners and a ten-millimeter nylon rope. The wind pushed and pulled at her from all sides with an icy insistence. That uneasy feeling in her gut was still there, worse than ever, as if its source had grown in strength.

Hesitantly, she made a move that she wouldn't have thought twice about in the gym, but as she slowly inched her way off small crimps to a large jug, her palms were sweating, and her exposed fingertips were nearly numb from the cold granite. As soon as her hand found a solid hold, she locked her fingers onto it like a vice and established herself. She rifled through the gear on her belt and selected her red number one. *The first clip is always the most dangerous. After this, you're protected. Relax, and clip.*

Snagging the red cam and jamming it hurriedly into a crack before her, she gave it a hard tug to check it would hold, then clipped in and let out the breath she'd been suppressing. She leaned into the wall and inhaled deeply a few times, then looked up at the climb ahead. *I'm a damn wreck today.* She wanted to do this. She needed to do it. She formulated a plan, envisioning herself moving up the route, picturing her hands grasping each hold, her feet hitting each edge, rail, crack, and nub. When Quinn started again, she felt the persistent tug of gravity against her back, beckoning her to the planet below.

Her feet stepped up. She focused on her toe hitting the foothold and shifted her hips and body with each progressive move. The goal was to maximize the weight over her legs so she could shift her arms from weight-bearing positions to those of balance and stability. *Think about the climbing, not the falling.* Each time she reached a suitable place for protection, she would clatter and clink through her gear, her nerves ratcheting up and her muscles quivering, but she managed. Somehow, she never fell.

Quinn continued, slowly, methodically, and timidly. *Greg always makes this look so easy.* His infuriating habit of being good at everything had irritated her more than once. She had to work hard and commit and struggle. He just sort of wandered through life. She knew being annoyed wasn't fair but she couldn't help it.

After about forty minutes, Quinn reached the end of the pitch. The anchor chains that had been placed by the original route setters were situated on a good ledge and looked sturdy, despite their age. She clipped into them, and once she was secure, she signaled Greg to start climbing, and he began his ascent.

She smiled as she watched him. When she climbed, she felt like she was swimming against the current, battling with the rock for position. When Greg climbed, he looked like he was floating, gently drifting downstream. He breathed steadily and moved with efficient, practical grace. She pulled up the slack and tightened the rope through her ATC as he made a speedy ascent toward her.

Quinn looked at the large bulge above that humped out from the face, leading to an off-width crack. The crack was too wide to jam hands and feet, and too small for an entire body to shimmy into like a chimney climb.

I'm glad he's leading that, not me. In less than half the time it had taken Quinn, he was on the ledge, high-fiving her. They exchanged gear, and he looked up with a countenance of all-encompassing focus.

"Good luck," she said, patting his shoulder. Greg's gaze never left the rock face.

He got up to the base of the bulge quickly, placing two pieces of gear at the bottom. One was to catch him if he fell early and one to back it up, in case his movements up and away from the wall dislodged the first. Greg tugged hard. The gear held. He continued. Out and upside down he went. He threw up his left foot and hooked his heel on a lip above him, then jutted his hand into the bottom of the off-width crack. Huffing out a deep breath, he levered hard on his left leg and hand, his other hand inching along as he slowly pulled himself vertical. He finally got his other hand into the crack, but as he weighted the hold, he popped right out. "Shit!" he shouted as he fell.

Quinn sucked up as much slack as she could and locked her brake hand down. Greg plummeted toward the ground until the rope went tight. She lurched two feet into the air, while he bounced to a stop.

Cursing, he kicked off the wall, and with the returning momentum, snagged a large hold and pulled himself back on route. He rested, shaking out his arms and flexing his fingers. "These holds suck!" he called down to Quinn as she hung suspended by the rope.

"You good?" she asked.

"Yeah," he replied. "Got a really good pro there, so I'm nice and safe. There's just nothin' up there," he continued. She simply nodded, unsure of how much insight she could offer. Pushing out from the wall with his legs, he hung on his belay and craned his neck up to survey the crack. He tried the same move with his leg but changed up his hand positions. Down he fell. Up she popped.

"FUCK!" he yelled. A moment of hanging, some deep focusing breaths, climbing, then falling again. "UGH!" He slammed his hand into his leg and kicked himself back again to grab the wall. Up and down they went a few more times until, finally, with monumental effort and a cry of exertion, Greg hauled himself up over the bulging off-width and got his right foot into the crack.

"Come on, man! You got it! Stand up!" Quinn encouraged him. She was jumping up and down, giddy with energy as she watched Greg push down on his right leg, bumping his left foot a little farther up the wall, followed by his left hand. He jammed both his arms into the crack, using opposing force to hold him in place, then stuck his right leg into the crack up to his thigh. Once his leg was secure, he took a large number five cam and wedged it in. Quickly, he snatched the rope and clipped it into the pro, putting his forehead against the face of the mountain and breathing heavily. After a moment of rest, he looked up the wall again, planning his next move.

"Good job, Greg!" Quinn shouted, despite the minute probability that he could hear her. Shivering involuntarily, she huddled closer to the wall in an attempt to escape from the ceaseless frigid alpine winds. The snow shimmered in the bright sunlight, creating a mystical veil about them, as if they were ascending through the clouds themselves. *Before the end of the day, we will be.* As terrifying as it could be, reaching the summit always swelled her with joy and feelings of accomplishment. She was doing something that a lot of people wouldn't be brave enough to attempt.

She could no longer see Greg since he'd climbed through the off-width. It was difficult to gauge the amount of slack on the rope, but she continued going through the routines of belaying, over and over, growing a bit bored. Finally, she felt a sharp tug, as if Greg had either made a large move, perhaps onto his belay ledge, or he was trying to pull the rope up because he'd already set up his anchor.

"YOU SAFE?" There was no reply, and the rope stayed tight to the wall. Quinn let out a little slack to avoid short-roping him and leaned back on her anchor, allowing her muscles to relax. She looked down into the valley below and immediately wished that she hadn't. It was not the four hundred feet of open air between her and ground that terrified her. It was the figure standing at the base of the mountain, waving up at her, wearing a bright red jacket. The red sleeve waved again, and her stomach lurched at the strange jerking of its arm. It seemed so unnatural, inhuman.

That sensation was nothing compared to the utter panic she felt when it spoke.

"Hello?" The voice sounded hesitant, confused. Worst of all, it was soft, a mere whisper. The word drifted up to her like an errant leaf on a light autumn breeze. It was identical to the voice she had heard outside of their camp, down to the strange crackling-radio quality of it.

"Hello! Are you alright?" Quinn called down to the figure, knowing it would do no good. *Greg can't even hear me one pitch up.* The figure just stood there, motionless. She turned to the rockface and realized the rope was taught again. If Greg didn't have enough slack, she'd pull him right off the face. *He's still climbing, get your act together.* Still, she had no way of gauging his progress. He hadn't fallen for a while, so that was something. *Come on, Greg, get up there and get me up there with you.* The last place she wanted to be was alone on this tiny ledge with that creep lurking below. Not that he could climb up after her or anything. She looked back down and felt a jolt of fear. *Where'd he go?*

The gear and haul bag, which they had left behind, seemed to be in the same place, undisturbed. There wasn't much to steal. *So what the hell did it want?* She leaned back as far as her anchor would allow, and her blood went cold. The figure had not simply walked away: it had started to climb. It had topped a small overhang that was only two pitches down. Climbing that distance must have taken her and Greg three hours, and this climber had ascended it in what she could only guess were seconds. In her panicked state, all sense of time was utterly relative and hardly relevant. She screamed. The creature stopped, looked up at her, and did its terribly awkward wave again. Its entire arm jerked back and forth like the greeting of a poorly constructed doll.

"Hello?" it said, and she pulled herself close to her anchor, frantically looking for anything she could use to defend herself. *Shit, shit, shit...* A quick jerk on her belay loop, and the rope was tight again. She gave Greg some slack, and when she glanced down again, on the ledge, two pitches down, the figure went on all fours. It flexed its shoulders, and then, with a mighty surge of speed and power, leaped into the air, clearing another fifty vertical feet in a single move. It started climbing like a cat with terrible speed. Now Quinn could see the figure's face, or what was left of it.

He might have been handsome once. The left side of his face had the sharp, weather-worn features of a seasoned climber—dull blue eyes and the remnants of a black beard, now hanging in frayed, ragged tatters from his crooked chin and sunken cheek. The right side was caved in completely.

Frantically, she searched for her ice axe on the tiny ledge to which she was helplessly attached. She remembered to let out some slack before awkwardly working the long-handled axe from her pack, never letting go of the brake on her belay with her other hand. She could hear the man's breathing. He was getting closer and closer.

Quinn looked over her shoulder once more to judge the man's exact location, distance, and speed. He was only about ten feet away, and he was looking up at her. Even in the howling wind and clean, crisp air of the mountain heights, she could smell the stench emanating from him. He smelled of the grave, of rot and decay. He smiled, a horrific sight. On the right side of his face, only the top row of his teeth was visible. What was left of his mouth curved up into the familiar human gesture, revealing sharp, pointed teeth.

It was no man.

Quinn was paralyzed as she locked eyes with the creature. A primal fear awoke in her. She was like a rabbit, crouching still until the last moment, hoping it would not have to run, to hide a little longer. As the creature bent to the wall, flexing its shoulders, she stared, transfixed.

The creature leaped, hands outstretched, its sharp yellowed claws glinting in the sun. Quinn screamed in rage and terror. The creature had covered the distance between them in a single bound. Quinn swung the ice axe with all her might. She'd timed her downswing perfectly to collide with the caved-in side of the creature's face. The axe was wrenched from her grasp and remained stuck in its head as it fell to the ground. It never made a sound. The black-red blood from its rotting skull splattered onto the rock and ice near her. Quinn watched, her heart pounding in her chest like a battering ram, as the creature plummeted four hundred feet and landed with a crunching thud.

She was hyperventilating and hanging limply from her anchor, her belay hand instinctively clutching the rope, her brake hand absently feeding rope through the ATC. Her mind was elsewhere, dismayed by killing someone.

No, that was not someone, that was something. Something that wanted to hurt me. She knew that in her bones. That thing was demonic. She had had no choice but to defend herself.

"It's gone. It's dead, it's dead, it's dead," she told herself.

Her gaze was still firmly locked on the corpse below. A small red splash on the otherwise gray and white landscape. For a moment it lay motionless and crumpled. Then, it started moving again. *No, no, no, no, no,* Quinn thought, then continued out loud, "Oh shit, no, no, no... GREG!" knowing he would be unable to hear her. She, however, could hear the creature.

"Hello?" it asked. The horribly familiar timbre and pitch of the question hadn't altered a bit, floating unnaturally up to her, somehow at full volume yet still a whisper. She heard the voice in her mind, gut, and soul. It sent shivers up and down her spine like a panicked column of ants. Her muscles twitched, and she started to cry. As Quinn watched the figure below stand up to its full height, she felt like she was going into cardiac arrest. It stretched and snapped its body in a sickening fashion as if popping the bones and joints back into place. Her hand still gripped the rope, and Greg was still on belay, but in her panic, she had let far too much rope run.

Suddenly she heard Greg yell, "FALLING!" His voice was faint and distant but terribly clear, and she began pulling the rope through her ATC as quickly as possible. Before she could get much in, the rope was ripping up the wall as Greg plummeted. Quinn was wrenched into the air, and her helmet cracked loudly on the bulge above her before her anchor caught. The impact set her ears ringing. Her vision exploded into a dizzying panorama of starbursts and colorful dots. She swayed like a carcass on a meat hook awaiting the butcher.

The creature below began to climb.

ELLIE

Ellie burst out of the trees to the edge of the traditional low camp for the Southern Pickett cirque wall. They should be here. If they were, they weren't lost, but it would still mean something had gone wrong. She ran into the rocky campground where Greg's yellow nylon tent flapped in the wind. Scanning the camp, she realized the site had been ransacked. She stopped and crouched down, drawing her .44.

To someone who didn't know the hikers in question, the campground may not have looked out of the ordinary, but Ellie knew Greg. He was a complete slob about almost everything in his life. His truck was beat-up and filled with gas station food and marijuana dispensary packaging. She'd seen his room in the Nelson home; it was covered with posters, and clothing was strewn about with the carelessness that only a twenty-three-year-old male could muster. But climbing was different for Greg. He had chosen to *be* a climber in every sense of the word, and he treated each trip like a professional endeavor. Ellie had actually given him shit about how pristinely his tent had been organized, how meticulously he'd racked his gear, and how neat his pack always was. *He has some of his mother in him after all,* she had thought.

The campground Ellie was investigating now looked like Greg's room. The tent was open, and a zipper hung off loosely from the front door, as if it had been ripped hard enough to break it. Inside, his gear was strewn about, and his sleeping bag had a tear in it. The flaps at the back were wide open, allowing a view of the Terror Glacier and the cirque wall beyond. Through the tent, she could see the icy sheen of the walls glimmering white and gray as they towered above the blue-white plain of the ice below. Low-hanging clouds cast a thin veil over the glacier and obscured the lower face of Mt. Terror.

The fire still had the ghost of embers in its pit, and the faintest trail of smoke snaked its way up in a translucent stream. A pink sleeping bag had been dragged halfway out and lay on the rocks like a fish washed up on shore. Ellie inspected the scattered supplies. They looked to be completely intact. Most of the food was dehydrated, but there were a couple packages of jerky. An unopened bag of sunflower seeds and a small squeeze packet of strawberry jam were also in evidence. *No bear leaves that shit behind.*

After thoroughly examining the area, Ellie found two sets of footprints heading to the Terror. She lifted her eyes to see a path of pink garden flags designating a route across the treacherous ice. The fog that hung over it seemed to watch her, to invite her in. Resolved, she nodded and started out, following the flags into the icy mist. She knew the glacier well, and she was happy to see her godson had chosen a good trail, well clear of the crevasse field, which was more expansive on the western slope. Still, she felt in her gut that if she didn't find Greg soon, she wasn't going to find him at all. The sinister fear that no one would find *her* crept suddenly into her mind. Her grip tightened subconsciously on the pistol as she crunched out into the white abyss.

GREG

He felt like he was floating, weightless upon a glassy lake. All the world's sounds, even the wind which had heretofore been all encompassing, were gone. Everything was gone. Greg opened his eyes, but it seemed as though he was looking through a foggy lens, and it made him want to vomit. He closed them again. *Yeah, that's pretty pleasant.* Suspended in the air, he could feel the wall bumping softly against his back as the wind blew him around. He could feel but couldn't hear anything. He focused as hard as he could. Nothing. *I'm dreaming.*

The sheer face extended below Greg's dangling form. He probably looked like a spider who had passed out drunk while making its web. Through a delirious haze, he surveyed his surroundings. Nearly twenty feet above, his large number five cam was lodged firmly into the off-width crux that had been thoroughly thwarting his climbing attempts for the past hour. On his last try, it had completely spit him out. He was starting to understand what happened. But right then, he didn't think it mattered that much. *Everything is fine. I'm not dead.*

"Eg!" said a garbled voice. It sounded to him like someone was trying to shout at him through a tin can on a string. Faint, distant, difficult to hear. "Gre... eg!" the voice garbled, louder. "GREG!"

"Ah!" Greg shouted, as the sound finally burst into his eardrum, waking him from his drunken-spider state. He jerked his head up, and his helmet hit an overhanging piece of rock. It made a strange crunching sound as it bounced off the granite.

His hand flew up to his trusty Petzl helm, that had shielded his head during countless adventures into Washington's mountains. He touched it with the hesitance of a man inspecting a lethal wound. A large crack ran the length of the helmet's crest, and Greg knew for certain what had happened. *I took a whipper.* He opened his eyes again and winced in pain. But this time, he forced himself to keep them open. Looking up to see that his rope was still hanging through the purple carabiner, he knew he was safe to hang a moment. He also knew he'd fallen quite a distance.

"Quinn?" he asked, far too softly.

"GREG!" she shouted up again. *She sounds terrified. Something is wrong.* "GREG! ARE YOU OKAY?!" she shrieked, like an animal fleeing a predator. "GREG! PLEASE ANSWER ME!" Resisting a mighty urge to send his lunch earthbound, he looked down and shouted loudly.

"QUINN! I'M OK!" Just opening his mouth to vocalize sent lances into his cranium. He felt again like he was going to throw up. This time, he did. His eyes clenched shut, and his fists clamped tight as he ejected the contents of his stomach. His forceful vomiting sent a second wave of pain into the bruised jelly of his brain. Below, he saw Quinn hanging, stuck in belay position. She was waving up at him and shouting frantically, but he couldn't hear a word she was saying over the ringing in his ears and the relentless wind.

When he peered down at Quinn again, he saw something that he absolutely couldn't explain. It looked like there was another climber on the wall, but they had no rope and were moving extremely quickly. It looked as if the climber in red had already managed to clear the first pitch in seconds, a task that had taken them an hour.

Of course, they had been managing ropes and gear. This guy seemed to be free soloing the exceedingly difficult terrain, and fast. Even in his befuddled state, Greg knew it was impossible.

A cold chill crept up his spine, focusing his addled wits. By some primal instinct, he realized they were in mortal danger. If he didn't do something, the climber was going to reach his girlfriend in no time. Greg's intuition took over.

He kicked off the wall with all his might, propelling himself out from the route and into the open air before swinging back into the wall.

He was clumsy, and his hands were shaky, so it took a couple of tries for him to get a good hold, but he finally pulled himself tight to the face. He grabbed onto a jug and wedged half his body into the off-width, twisting his knee so that his thigh was pushing against one wall of the crack while his foot jammed into the other. Holding his body in place, he fumbled around his belt until he procured a suitably large piece of protection. He got the gear placed, checking back down on Quinn as he did so. The solo climber was still flying up the face at an unprecedented pace, scaling the face with the ease of a professional speed climber on a practiced route. *Fuck, fuck, fuck!* Greg thought as he frantically clove-hitched his rope into three pieces of gear. Moving with the speed and efficiency of endless repetition, he secured himself to the wall. Once he knew he was safe, he leaned out from the wall and called down to Quinn. Raising his hands and waving them frantically, he shouted, "SAFE, QUINN! OFF BELAY!" Then he rapidly hauled up the rope. "GET UP HERE, QUINN! CLIMB!"

QUINN

She didn't know when she'd started to cry, but the tears were flowing in a steady stream down her cheeks and freezing to her chin as she hung there, watching this crazed, red-coated beast approach, waiting for Greg to get her on belay.

The climber in pursuit had reached a ledge just twenty feet below, and it stopped to look up. Its smile was fixed, like the mouth on a plastic mask. She'd have thought it was a mask if not for the fact that she'd seen its glistening saliva. As it stood, she noticed that its shoulders were slightly uneven, giving it a hunched, leaning aspect; its neck was twisted sharply to the left.

Without moving its mouth in the slightest, it said, "Hello?" like a child asking if someone was in the basement in the middle of the night. It waved, jerking its arm back and forth. Quinn didn't even notice she'd wet herself. She turned toward the wall and started toward Greg. *He'll know what to do.* As she climbed, she didn't think about it, didn't even consider her moves, and she didn't contemplate falling. Falling was not an option.

Hastily, she scrambled until she reached the bulge section where Greg had struggled for so long. Mimicking his movements she'd seen from below, she threw up her heel to leverage her body into the crack above. She managed to lock in the heel hook and get a good hold on a jug at the bottom of the crack.

As soon as she reached the crack itself, she threw up a hand instinctively to catch a hold. No hold was there. Suddenly, she noticed the generous amount of slack.

She looked up and saw Greg pulling the rope hastily. He was trying to put her on belay, but there was fifteen feet of rope between them. Clinging to the jug with both hands, she searched frantically for another hold, something to pull her up and into the crack where the gravitational pull of the void beneath her would not be so present. She desperately needed to put whatever was climbing below her out of her line of sight. *If I could just...* She reached up again and stretched with all her might. From just below her, sounding as if it were whispering into her ear, she heard—

"Hello?"

ELLIE

Y*ep, fuck all of this,* Ellie thought as she traversed the fog-shrouded glacier. The serene, crystalline ice that greeted the sharp points of her crampons belied the harsh truth of the mountain world. *No matter how beautiful it looks, it's cold and hard and unfeeling.* The glacier was a most sinister manifestation of that empirical truth.

All around her, the world seemed soft, fluffy, gentle. A downy blanket of snow carpeted the ground ahead, behind, to either side, and even above on the jagged granite peaks, making them seem like steep, rolling hills. The ominous fog that clung to the large saddle wafted past in a wispy current, blown by a gentle westbound breeze. But every time one of her sharp steel crampon blades tromped down to the ground, they met the glacial ice that lurked beneath. It was as hard as stone and thrice as treacherous. For all Ellie knew, she could be walking on a shelf no thicker than a dinner plate below which could be a colossal cavern with a not-so-fluffy floor of jagged ice. *It's just a glacier, Ellie. You're starting to sound like those amateur adventurers you can't stand*, she chided herself.

As weird days went, Ellie didn't have any that could compare. Before today, she never would have believed something could top the day her chopper crashed on her second Iraq tour. She'd looked death in the face that day, seeing seven of her fellow soldiers scattered around. Buzzards had been circling over her when she opened her eyes. One had already started on Mark, a man she'd known since boot camp.

Watching buzzards pick apart a guy who could kick your ass at boxing, chess, and every other damned thing really gave you a sense of perspective where longevity and purpose were concerned.

In terms of longevity, the glacier had her thoroughly trounced. It had existed when dinosaurs were still cruising around. Whether those dinosaurs were wearing feathers or scales, the glacier was there, cutting through mountains, designing and redesigning the topography, and simply being some scary-ass ice. She felt she had a better purpose at least. *Find Greg and Quinn.*

Ellie looked like a Viking shield-maiden, clad as she was in her spiked shoes and thick red mountaineering attire, wielding an ice axe in one hand and a .44 revolver in the other. Her head scanned back and forth like a bird dog sniffing for pheasant. *Keep that gun handy. If I were some psycho fuck, I'd definitely have my lair up here*, she thought as she prodded the ground ahead before taking each step, following the path of pink flags.

She'd taught Greg the flag trick on one of their first outings together. She was glad to see it was a lesson he'd taken to heart. Anyone who didn't have a marked path would be walking completely blind no matter how straightforward a glacier crossing seemed. The landscape was deceptively flat, and aside from the mountains looming above, the ground was a uniform shade of white. Even in clear conditions, it would be easy to get off trail and wander onto a more hazardous area of the glacier. But with the silent mist, it was a near certainty. The only sound which reverberated through the crypt-like world of the fading alpine day was the methodical crunching of her crampons and the shaky wisps of breath that puffed out of her mouth with each soft, gentle exhalation.

Like a gun shot, something rang through the saddle.

"*Greg!*" a female voice echoed across the glacier. The voice was quiet, but the tone was panicked, terror-filled, and desperate. Ellie stopped immediately.

"GREG!" Ellie screamed through the misty shroud enveloping her. "QUINN? THAT YOU?"

"Greg! Are you okay?" rang out, a little louder, sounding like Quinn. Without further hesitation, Ellie pointed toward the voice and ran blindly across the Terror. Labored breathing, crunching boots, clicking spikes, the occasional skid, grunts of pain and exertion, and her heart pounding all shattered the silence around her. *Quinn. that's gotta be Quinn calling for Greg, calling for help, calling to see if he's okay.* Then, as suddenly as the sound had started, it stopped.

GREG

She'd just gasped. It was soft, slightly questioning, as if she didn't even know it was a question or an answer. It was the last sound Greg heard her make. She hadn't screamed; just a short, surprised gasp. Then she was gone. He'd gotten as much rope up as he could, and upon seeing she was about to fall, thrown on a quick body belay, but there had still been a good amount of rope between them. He couldn't believe it when he'd seen her climb over the bulge with ten feet of slack at her waist. She was a timid climber, yet there she'd been, climbing free, off belay, on probably the hardest pitch she'd ever attempted, without even seeing the route she was undertaking.

No wonder she fell. The comment slipped into his psyche without consent. Whatever she'd seen had scared the fear of falling right out of her. It must have scared her so badly she'd denied her intrinsic nature. *That fucker in red. Where did he go?*

Quinn was gone. Not just fallen, but gone, gone. She'd begun to free fall, but when the rope snapped taut, she'd stopped. The force had ripped Greg headfirst into the wall, sending violent tremors quaking through his head in pulsing, steady waves. His jaw had slammed shut, forcing his teeth into his tongue so hard that he tasted blood. He'd wondered if he'd actually bitten a chunk off.

All thoughts of himself ceased when he looked down to see Quinn swinging in and out of his line of sight, dangling below the bulge. Out and in she swung, once, twice, and then, to Greg's horror, the weight on the other end of the rope vanished.

He fell onto his personal anchor system, which caught him with a rough jerk. He peered down again. Where Quinn had been, there was only a severed rope. She and the person in red were gone. The mists gathered below, and Greg was alone.

He didn't know if the tears in his eyes were from the terror of being trapped, the grief for his lost girlfriend, or the excruciating pain in his head that increased its intensity with every wracking sob. Greg vomited into the void again and hung there, quivering in the chill mountain air, as useless as his rope. Leaning backward and unclipping his helmet, he let the cracked plastic fall. As it tumbled to the snowy earth below, the pressure on his head subsided. Mechanically, he began hauling up the remaining meters of his prized seventy-meter orange Mammut rope that had saved his life more times than any person or seatbelt ever did.

Crying, he pulled the now feather-light rope up and flaked it over his leg in alternating loops, just like Ellie had taught him. He thought about her, her lessons about survival, the stories she shared about the horrors of war and the wild, and of the stories he knew she had but couldn't bring herself to share. He wished she were there now, but he was as alone as was possible for a human being—a young man, perched on a razor's edge between the realms of death and life. Hundreds of feet above safety and a thousand feet below it. All he had to save himself was a full rack, designed for climbing with a partner, and a severed, frayed rope. He knew that to descend via rappel, he would need two seventy-meter ropes. One forty was not going to cut it.

The rope! he suddenly thought. Their extra gear, which they'd brought in case they had to spend the night on the mountain, was two pitches down. Greg only had to find a way down. He surveyed what remained of his rack. It would mean sacrificing his remaining gear to make the descent; a small price to pay for his life.

He tied the frayed end into a tight barrel knot to make sure it wasn't going to unravel or allow him to slide off the end and plummet to the ground below. Taking the rope from his waist, he lashed another barrel knot on the opposite end, looped both strands through his belay device, and locked the rappel setup with a carabiner. Below his device, he fastened the ropes onto his safety Prusik knot and gripped it with his right hand.

Breath puffing out in stifled sobs, hands shaking, he glided down to where he'd last seen Quinn. Greg didn't think he could handle seeing her dead, splattered on the ground, but no matter how it would make him feel, he had to face it. She would have risked anything to save him. She'd started climbing because of him in the first place. It had taken years for her to become even partially comfortable with it, and now she might have died by way of her worst fear. Greg began to cry again.

He was forced to build four anchors, two of which were extremely sketchy, just to reach the ledge marking the start of the second pitch. By now, his gear was almost entirely in the face above him. With a natural anchor on the ledge, he could expend his remaining gear on his final anchor, which, with both ropes tied together, might be enough to get him back to the ground, but as he looked to the small tight corner where they had stashed their bag, it was gone. The rope had gone.

Quinn had gone. *Everything* was gone. He looked over the ledge to the bottom of the climb to see that the haul bag had fallen two pitches down to the base. It must have gotten knocked off the ledge by Quinn or that red-coated bastard. Without that second rope, or more gear, Greg wasn't going anywhere.

In frustration, he slammed his head into the wall. An admittedly stupid habit he'd developed over the years. When he was thrashing around on a pitch, he'd headbutt the rock. Usually, when he executed this neanderthal maneuver, he had the protection of a helmet. Not this time. Greg hadn't considered his discarded helmet or his concussion. As soon as his head met rock, everything went black.

ELLIE

Ellie finally stepped off the glacier. She was only a short walk from the base of a climbing line. The gear was still assembled for a haul, stretching up the wall. Above, she saw a limp figure, clad in a lime green jacket. She started to run.

"GREG!" she shouted through her heavy breathing. "GREG! GREG! YOU OKAY, KID?"

He said nothing.

The sun was beginning to dip below the western horizon. At this point, Ellie reckoned they had mere hours of daylight left. *I'm gonna have to work fast.* The bitter cold air shot into her lungs, making her chest ache, but she got to the base quickly. As she looked at Greg's line, the sickening feeling she'd felt at the campsite came rushing back. She bent over his haul bag and examined it. Removing her cap and jacket, she attempted to quell the sweat that was threatening to rush from her pores. Sweating at high altitude was an easy way to catch hypothermia, and an easy way to die.

The bag was well packed, as usual. In it was emergency overnight gear, which would have allowed Greg and Quinn to attach themselves to the wall in a nylon cocoon if they weren't able to finish the climb in one day. There was a seventy-meter climbing rope, a Jet Boil, dehydrated meals, tea, and high-altitude toiletries—empty Gatorade bottles, hand sanitizer, toilet paper. *Hand sanitizer? So Greg's girlfriend was definitely here. Where is she now?*

She traced the haul line up and realized it was not attached to the wall. The rope was simply caught in a rock feature. When Ellie gave it a tug, it tumbled down. She caught the end and thought, *You better be alive, Greg. You still owe me a beer.*

At a glance, she could tell the seventy-meter rope in Greg's bag had only been used a handful of times. She knew what she had to do. As she donned her harness, she checked for any twists or bends, then racked up all the climbing gear she thought she would need: belay devices, a set of cams, ascenders, runners, and webbing. She dumped out her pack and coiled the rope methodically into her bag. After setting up a soloing system, she started the pitch, and the rope spooled out of her pack with a reassuring whisper.

* * *

When Ellie reached her godson, dangly limply from the face of the cliff, she immediately felt hot tears running from her eyes to freeze on her cheeks.

"Greg? Greg, you okay, hon? Talk to me, dumbass! Why are you up here alone?"

Greg said nothing, but Ellie could see his chest slightly rising. She pulled down the gaiter protecting his neck to feel for a pulse, her fingers shaking as if she'd just climbed seventeen pitches. As soon as she felt the steady *thump, thump, thump* of his healthy heartbeat, she calmed. *He's alive. Relax and do what you need to do.*

She rescued him like she had so many others. Doing it alone was no easy task, but she successfully finished load-hauling his body to the base of the mountain, repelled down to him, then load-hauled him again. By the time they were both safely at the bottom, the sun had made its final retreat, leaving only its residual pink-and-yellow atmospheric light. Upon reaching the ground, Ellie made a quick decision to sledge Greg back to his camp and get him warm as soon as possible.

She dug through her supplies for her sleeping pad and opened its self-inflating valves. Grabbing a piece of ripstop fabric from Greg's bag, she lashed a long length of webbing to the end. Then she attached the fabric to the bottom of the sleeping pad and laid Greg on it. Using the remaining webbing to secure him to the pad, she left room for handles. She dumped the rope from her pack and refilled it with her essential gear: first aid kit, cooking supplies, water, jacket. Onto her stiff-soled mountaineering boots, she strapped her crampons. Gloved hands gripped the webbing of the makeshift sledge. It was clunky and heavy, but it slid. Clicking her headlamp on, she set off across the glacier with grim determination, following the trail of pink garden flags that led out across the snowy expanse.

At least the damn fog has gone, she thought as she trudged ahead. She could vaguely see Greg's neon yellow tent against the stark gray and whites of the alpine saddle. Unable to drag the sledge with one hand, she couldn't test the ice and had to rely on sight to avoid crevasses. She was looking down for sections of snow which seemed too loose or too blue. Every couple of seconds, she glanced up to make sure she hadn't strayed from the flag path.

Then she stopped. The path had been heading in the right direction when she started, but now, the wind was blowing directly into Ellie's face. *I shouldn't be heading west...* Ellie shook her head. *The fog was everywhere, and you were running. Keep following the flags, and you'll be fine. The ground is sound.* She thought about all the pessimistic things she'd said about people getting lost hiking because they overreacted easily, yet there she was, panicking at the first sign of uncertainty. Her doubts remained the same. The utter lack of sound seemed to join her heart tremors in warning. *You're going the wrong way.*

Danger, whispered the stalking cat in the back of her mind.

Frantic, Ellie stopped and looked around. She could have sworn she heard... her radio crackling at her hip? She was sure she had left it off, and even if it was on, who could hail her up here? She put the radio to her lips, "That you, Lynn?" The radio gave no answer, not even static. It was dead. *So where the hell did that come from?* She surveyed her surroundings again. Now she was certain she no longer had any idea where the tent was. *What the fuck?*

"Hello?" the voice crackled, as if coming through her transmitter, but it sounded distant, and it definitely didn't come from her hip. It seemed to come from a small snowy bluff that loomed in front of her. The pink garden flags led up and over it. She was convinced she hadn't crossed that feature last time, and despite its sloped shape, she knew the bluff was almost certainly a precarious cornice, overhanging a crevasse. *Why would anyone have moved those flags?*

"Hello?" asked a man's voice with the inflection of a child checking under their bed for the bogeyman.

"Hello?" the weak and pained voice came from behind her. Ellie whirled to see Greg try to sit up, but he immediately fell back onto the sled with a groan. "Where am I?" he asked through clenched teeth. She barely heard him breathe out the words, "Where's Quinn?"

Without thinking, Ellie knelt beside him and began asking him questions, opening up her first aid kit as she did, and handed him her water bladder.

GREG

Greg's head throbbed as he opened his eyes. He squinted up to see Ellie kneeling above him, saying something. Her lips moved, but it was like she was talking to him from inside an aquarium. Nothing was getting through. His head swam when she leaned in close and snapped her fingers once... twice... three times.

"GREG!" she shouted. He finally heard her and tried to sit up, but a gentle hand restrained him. She embraced him in a hug, not too rough, but hard, as if she was trying to transfer some of her life force into him. With her mouth right next to his ear, he could tell she was crying. He had never seen her cry.

"Aunt Ellie?" he asked weakly, "Where?" She just proffered him a water bladder and nodded.

The liquid was divine. As it ran down his throat, it was not a mere thirst-quenching drink. It was a drink that reminded him he was alive. A drink that breathed perceivable existence back into his muscles. The bellows of his lungs expanded and contracted more smoothly, and his heart felt less labored. *Why is Aunt Ellie here? Where is here?*

He took another drink of water, greedily sucking the liquid down. To him, it tasted of family and life and love. *Love?* he thought, glancing around, disoriented. "Where's Quinn?"

"I was hoping you'd know that."

"Quinn," Greg said, matter-of-factly. "She hates glaciers."

Ellie seemed concerned. Her speech was slow and precise, as if she were speaking to a child. Greg was far too dulled to take offense.

"Where's Quinn? When did you last see her? Can you tell me anything about what happened?"

Greg nodded, taking a moment to grasp his drifting thoughts. *Where did I see her last? We'd been climbing. We'd argued about gear checks, then...*

A gasp came from somewhere near them, soft, slightly questioning, a distinctly human sound of surprise.

A prologue to panic.

They both snapped their heads toward the sound, but all Greg saw was snow drifting lazily over the icy ground in whimsical wisps. The world grew darker and colder by the second, and he shivered. Turning to Ellie, he noticed she was standing with her hand on her gun.

"Quinn! You out there, hon?" she called into the eerie winter night. "It's Ellie. I'm here to help you. I've got Greg with me!"

He heard the gasp again, as if far off. It sounded eerily familiar. "That's not her." He knew, somehow. He just knew that something was wrong, undeniably and lethally wrong.

Ellie tightened her grip on her gun and took up her long-handled ice axe. Prodding the ground, she walked carefully on the treacherous ice. Greg attempted to rise and go with her, then realized he was lashed to the sledge. When he moved, the swimming sensation returned, and pain exploded in his head.

"Aunt Ellie..." he said through the sharp pains, thrashing against the webbing around his chest and arms. "Untie me."

She stopped and went back to him, double-checking every step with the sharp steel spike at the bottom of her axe. She released the hammer of the gun and holstered it for a moment to untie him.

"Somebody's out there, Greg." Her expression was serious. "Somebody pretty fucked up. I found some shit on the way up here that had me worried you were already dead. Have you seen anything weird?"

"No," he replied automatically, but then he thought back. "Quinn was acting strange. And the other night..." he paused. Ellie urged him on. "We heard somebody," he said slowly.

Ellie's eyebrows knitted. "Heard what?"

"Just a voice. Coming from a radio, like that gasp we just heard. It said hello." Greg tried to stand again, but Ellie gently stopped him.

"You need to stay here. I have no idea how serious your injuries are, but you definitely have a concussion. Lie there on your back, drink as much water as you need, and don't go to sleep." She fumbled in her pack and pulled out a granola bar and three red pills from her first aid kit. "Eat this, then take these," she said, handing him the bar and pain pills. "Don't try to stand up. Your leg is fucked." She gave him a reassuring shoulder pat, then stood.

"I'm scared," he said, shocked at how helpless and childlike he sounded. It had leaped from his subconscious to his mouth without passing any of the usual sensors. Ellie paused. A strange look was in her eyes as they locked onto his.

“Yeah, me too,” she admitted. The fact that she was afraid made Greg feel worse. “Stay here, kid, I’ll be right back.” His godmother turned away and again made her way out onto the glacier.

Greg ate a few bites of the granola bar but found it difficult: chewing hurt too much. He swallowed the pills and stowed the bar for later, drinking more water and laying back. Hearing Ellie’s boots crunching farther away, he asked, “Aunt Ellie?”

“Yeah?”

“Yell to me if you find her?”

“I’ll bring her straight back.”

ELLIE

Ellen Jensen, veteran of Desert Storm and rescuer of over two hundred lost outdoorsmen and women, traversed her favorite glacial valley feeling as if she were on the ocean floor. For the past decade, the mountains had been the only place in which Ellie truly felt at home, but today she felt as if she didn't belong. She had a sense that indomitable predators lurked around her. Ellie knew she was being hunted ever since Greg had stated, "That wasn't her."

So, it's some bear-skinnin' hillbilly with a hell of a falsetto. You ain't skinnin' me. On her next step, the snow crunched aside to reveal the deep, dark ice below. Her spikes bit deeply for purchase as she continued forward, following the path of flags.

The flatness of the plain gave way to a small overhang, revealing a large depression in the glacial ice. In its center ran a large crack, wide enough to drop a car in. The crevasse emanated a resonant, deep cerulean blue from its hypogean depths. In front of the crack were the rest of the flags.

They stuck out, bent and twisted and arranged to form the same symbol she'd seen with the bear's blood and entrails. Central to the symbol was a figure in a red coat, lying face down. The gentle breeze rustled a bit of torn coat loose and blew it down the gaping crack behind the body. Ellie dropped to a crouch and surveyed the scene, her pistol at the ready. The body looked familiar, but she couldn't put her finger on why.

She crept forward, her head on the swivel, constantly checking her three, her nine, and glancing over her shoulder at her six. The unmistakable stench of death clung to the air, growing more pungent as she neared the crevasse. The body before her, frozen solid as it was, could not equal the wretched smell. Ellie knew she was in a precarious position. Cold sweat burst from her pores, and every hair on her body stood at attention.

With her pistol trained on the center of its back, she prodded the corpse with her boot and fought the urge to plug her nose. She wanted to keep the axe handy, even though the body was stiff and unresponsive. At least it hadn't been crucified and mutilated like the bears. She kicked it again, harder, keeping her gun on target. It didn't move. No rise and fall of breath. No signs of life whatsoever, yet signs of death were everywhere. Torn clothing, blood on his cheek and hands—dried and mingling with frost-bite-black extremities. After another compulsory glance around and a few more seconds waiting to see if it breathed, she pushed hard with her foot on the figure's torso, turning it over.

Shit, she thought, dropping her shoulders. *Travis something.* The coat had looked familiar, and battered and torn as the face was, she knew it from the poster in her office. He'd been missing for nearly two months, assumed to have fallen down a crevasse.

She heard a *crunch, crunch* behind her.

Ellie whirled to see a short young woman standing there. She was thin and pale with dull green eyes, one of which was severely blackened, as if she'd been hit by rock or a particularly large fist. Her head was cocked at an awkward angle as she stared at Ellie, saying nothing.

Her lips were drawn back into a too-large smile. She wore a bright purple down jacket and black climbing pants. Around her waist was a climbing harness, from which was tied a length of Greg's orange rope that dangled into the crevasse.

The girl made the same curious gasp Ellie had heard earlier. Her stomach lurched, and she pointed her gun at the girl when she started to approach with grotesque, shambling steps like she was walking on stilts, unable to bend her legs. Her feet were bent out at sickening angles, and her ankles bore her weight as she staggered forward. As a SAR agent, Ellie had seen cases where the extremely wounded were able to accomplish incredible feats fueled by pure adrenaline, but it didn't seem adrenaline was propelling this girl. It was unnatural. Evil.

"Quinn," Ellie tried to sound relieved. "Are you alright?"

The figure continued forward, slowly. About twenty feet away, she gave her little gasp in response.

"Don't come any closer," Ellie commanded, raising her gun and aiming it at the girl. "I'm out here to help you and Greg, but I don't like the way you're looking at me. Now, do you remember me or not?"

The girl paused. Her smile, seemingly frozen on her face, evaporated to be replaced by a determined grimace, then transformed into other expressions. Shock. Recognition. Pained sorrow. And finally, back to a smile, sweet and loving, not too big and not too small. The girl blankly stared at her; the new smile fixed on her face like an image on a forgotten television screen. She seemed to be waiting for approval.

Ellie's bullet fired into the air with a cracking boom. It shattered the silence of the high mountain world. Quinn, or the thing that looked like her, didn't even blink.

"I'm not fuckin' around. Talk to me, and we can all go home. But if you come any closer without talkin', I'll shoot in your direction."

The Quinn thing started running, shambling, and she was devilishly fast. Ellie barely had time to get off the shot.

The bullet flew harmlessly over Quinn's head as it fell to all fours and leaped. The slight girl collided with Ellie, bearing all the force of an avalanche. Ellie heard a sickening crack and wondered if it was one of her bones or the ice beneath them preparing to give way. The gun clattered uselessly from her hand and slid across the ice before dropping down into the gap and out of sight. Ellie's left hand swung up viciously with the ice axe, but the small girl was quick and freakishly strong.

The Quinn thing caught Ellie's hand in her small purple glove and wrenched it so hard Ellie felt her bones snap. The ice axe dropped from her weak, useless fingers, and her head swam with the shock. Fingers that had pulled Ellie up countless rock faces, had jammed into hundreds of cracks and lifted her entire body weight over and over through a lifetime of cruxes, now lacked the strength to open or close. Her legs, that had walked everywhere from the dust-swept streets of war-torn Iraq to the top of Mt. Rainer, were jelly. Her well-muscled arms and core were completely pinned by the incomprehensible strength of this five-feet-two form that was now looking down on her with a terrible, creepy smile. As Ellie peered up at the creature, she knew she was staring at the face of death.

The girl's eyes were green, once sparkling and enchanting in life, now glossed over with the thin veil that shrouded the eyes of the deceased. Her twisted neck revealed a fatal break, and the stench that had wafted out from the crevasse clung onto this figure. Up close, Quinn's teeth seemed a little sharper than natural, as if they'd been filed and honed for rending and tearing flesh. The girl perched atop Ellie, opened her mouth inhumanly wide, and descended on Ellie's face.

Ellie screamed and thrashed. Fight as she might, there was absolutely nothing she could do. Her scream, as well as her head, was swallowed by the monster that looked like Quinn.

THE ANCIENT ONE

Quinn was the name of this skin. The Ancient One found it rather unique. It was a name it'd never heard a skin called before, and it'd been taking skins for a very long time. The skin was beautiful. The Ancient One was always pleased when it captured one like this. It made the gathering of future prey easier, especially human males. The Ancient One wondered why more of its kind didn't live in the high places. Prey was relatively abundant, often alone, usually fit, and well cared for. In the lower world of stinking cities and the black tar rivers full of flying, honking metal, humans had grown fat, lazy, and disgusting.

Up here, only superb specimens could survive. More and more prey had been arriving every year. The strong skins came to indulge in their masochistic ambitions, and when they were finished scampering on rocks, splashing in the waters, and rutting in their colorful dens, they were easy prey. The Ancient One had gathered many skins this year, and with them their memories. If it chose to, it could descend from the mountain and track down the humans dear to them. Those they loved were always the easiest prey: trusting, worried, desperate. Once the Ancient One had devoured their essences, it could bring their skins to the crevasse, and its collection would grow.

The Ancient One dropped into its lair, carrying its two new prizes. It jammed its long, protruding claws into the ice walls as it stepped deeper and deeper into the glacial cave. The reflections of the two limp bodies slung over its shoulders danced off the subterranean house of mirrors. At the bottom of the cave, the Quinn-skin's boots sloshed through a shallow arctic pool as the small form hauled the skins called Greg and Ellie into a larger chamber, a horrid cathedral of ice and blood. Hanging from the walls were several skins, dressed as bikers, backpackers, climbers, kayakers, and other such prey that ventured into the high places. Men and women alike hung, slaughtered. Under each, painted in blood, was the ceremonial symbol of the Ancient One. Each body was opened from groin to throat, empty of vital organs. The Ancient One only needed the skins. The rest it devoured.

It gasped softly. The last sound of the human Quinn, and the only vocalization it could use in her skin. It wished it would have gotten words from this one; it was such a pretty skin. But even without them, it would still be useful. From the other female skin, it had absorbed a terrified scream. Many of its skins screamed, but hers was another pretty skin, so it was valuable. From the boy, it had gotten a few human words. He'd been dead when the Quinn-skin had made its way over to him, but when the Ancient One gathered his skin, it'd felt the words, hot, despairing, and delicious on its mind.

"Help me... please."

The boy had died weeping, speaking softly to himself. Yes, that sort of human talk was useful for trapping prey.

The Ancient One began readying the skins for future use. One at a time, it disemboweled them and discarded their innards for later consumption. After it hung them, it painted the symbol beneath them with their blood and then looked up at its menagerie of human disguises.

The Ancient One would eat well this winter.

NOTE FROM THE AUTHOR

Hey there reader, thanks so much for reading my debut novella, *Crevasse*. I hope you enjoyed it as much as I did writing it.

If you're worried there's nothing else for you to read, never fear! I have quite a few published short stories featured on the popular indie publishing sites Wattpad and Simily. These shorts are also in the horror genre; I do think you'd enjoy them.

Additionally, I have a newsletter that I release twice monthly. That letter includes exclusive 'Beta Reader' access to my fantasy serial Real Heroes on a Real Quest, as well as regular updates for upcoming content for both my writing and the podcast.

Finally, I'd like to humbly request that you leave a review for this novella. Reviews are vastly important to an author, as they help with social proof of the stories' quality, ranking on Amazon, and most importantly, show me what my readers think of my writing, where I can improve, and what I should keep on doing.

Scan any of the corresponding codes on the next page to support me in these endeavors and to satisfy your craving for more Clay Vermulm fiction. Thank you again for being here. I'd love to hear from you via the contact form on my website.

Sincerely,
Clay Vermulm

NEWSLETTER SIGN-UP

Sign up for the newsletter and contact Clay directly at the Clay Vermulm Fiction Website:

To read Clay's other work, check out Wattpad and Simily:

ABOUT CLAY VERMULM

The no-fall zone—the point on a climb where falling means death and finishing the route to the top is safer than attempting a descent.

As a man who climbs and explores the mountains regularly, author Clay Vermulm is no stranger to arguably insane amounts of risk. After all, what sane man would forsake a teaching career and a profitable position as a restaurant sous chef to become a full-time author?

Sanity notwithstanding, that is exactly what Clay has done. Rather than continue to put his passion on hold while slogging through a career path for which he feels no true exultation, he decided to embark fully down the path of writing narrative fiction.

Since 2020, Clay has been a finalist for the Rick D. Moranis short story competition. His work has been published on the *Miss Fearsome* YouTube channel, Substack, Simily, and on his website, clayvermulmfiction.com. Clay also hosts a podcast called *Sinister Soup*, devoted to promoting his fellow newly published and independent authors of genre fiction.

ACKNOWLEDGEMENTS

Thank you to all of you who have read my work so far and kept me moving along on this author journey. I want to give a special thanks to those of you who actively contributed to the publishing of this novella.

First, thank you my editors, Kristen Noland, Philip Ridgers, Adina Edelman, and Pauline Harris. Many thanks also to my cover designer, Meike Haakart (Art of Maquenda) for her brilliant design.

My sincere thanks go to my beta readers, Jake and Kyle Love, Wallace Bossie, Aaron Toney, Konrad Shroeder, Deanna Leatherman, Kendra Vermulm, and Travis Vermulm.

Made in the USA
Las Vegas, NV
14 October 2023